M000248757

Still Life

A LOVE STORY

ELIZABETH COOKE

Elizabeth Cooke

abbott press

Cover Painting:
"Neuilly Flower Market," Menpes, Mortimore Ludington (1855-1938)-Private Collection-© Look and Learn-Bridgeman Images

Abbott Press books may be ordered through booksellers or by contacting:

Abbott Press
1663 Liberty Drive
Bloomington, IN 47403
www.abbottpress.com
Phone: 1 (866) 697-5310

ISBN: 978-1-4582-2043-1 (sc)
ISBN: 978-1-4582-2042-4 (hc)
ISBN: 978-1-4582-2041-7 (e)

Library of Congress Control Number: 2016917624

Print information available on the last page.

Abbott Press rev. date: 03/25/2022

Contents

Part One

Part Two

Part Three

Part One

1927 January Paris

GALERIES LAFAYETTE

1.

It is hard to define the line where dreams begin, especially in the mists of Paris, on a Sunday in January 1927. I am 17, a girl with a gentle face, made softer by those Paris mists, where frost in the air obscures all edges.

My hair is straight and blonde, cut in Dutch boy fashion, and I am wearing a Breton hat with red ribbons down the back. I have on my favorite dark green, wool Sunday suit, with black stockings and high-laced boots, looking the proper schoolgirl to passers-by, as I gaze longingly into the windows of Galeries Lafayette.

Galeries Lafayette is not an art emporium. It is Paris' only department store where one can buy a pot or a sweater, even soap. It is a rarity in Paris to have everything in one shop. How much more sensible than to have to buy each item in a separate store, less tiring.

I gaze at a particularly intriguing new coffee machine in the front of the window. It is polished and gleaming and different from the usual *filtre* used to make coffee at home. Probably from America.

My name is Camille de St. Phalle, and I am the only child of an insurance broker. I go to the Lycée d'Athènes for young women on the corner of rue Monsieur, an elegantly risqué name for a street, about which my co-students love to giggle. I hopefully will finish with the

Lycée early in the summer, providing I survive a set of examinations, the thought of which already chills me.

Rue Monsieur is on the left bank of the Seine, behind Les Invalides, Napoléon's massive tomb and tourist attraction, and only a block from the Musée Rodin which is housed in the beautiful Hôtel Biron, adjoining rue de Varenne. The next street is rue Monsieur and my school.

To me, the Musée Rodin, in that wonderful old building, has a wickedness that delights. Perhaps the great sculptor's obsession with women, old and young, makes me feel this way. It is said he had naked models all over the studio, and he liked to lie in wait, sketch book at the ready to catch them in some spontaneous pose that, in turn, kicked off an idea for a composition lying asleep in his mind.

I am not much educated in art, but I am aware in Rodin's day (the 1880s and '90s particularly – although he did not die until toward the end of the Great War), it was the custom for artists to pose their models carefully, in contrived positions. With Rodin, he watched them freely – did not pose them at all. They combed their hair or read or rubbed one another's backs. Then he would pounce with his pencil, drawing studies to be translated into clay and marble and bronze. They say he often pounced with something other than his pencil!

It is one of my secrets to visit the Musée Rodin, pretending I am 18 and of an age to view Rodin's statues of naked men and women and couples kissing. The loving couples – like Eternal Spring – he did that in 1884 and the youthful figures are alive, with vibrant limbs as pliant as spring branches full of sap.

Rodin's Fugit Amor- that was done a year later, I think, where the young couple, lying on a block of stone that could be their bed of passion, evoke the evanescence of love. The girl, hands to her head, is literally slipping through the young man's fingers. He holds her by one breast, but she will escape him and love will be gone. The girl is regretful, gliding out from beneath the weight of the young man, leaving his body exposed.

Why do I tremble before the sculptures, tingle with the fear of being caught, when Suzelle Mauldre, my dearest friend, and I sneak to the Musée Rodin? Maman would be horrified. 'Totally inappropriate for a young girl!' she would say. If she knew! I purse my lips feeling a line of droplets on my upper lip, deposited there by the wet mist.

Perhaps I am fascinated because the love of Rodin's life was another young girl with the name 'Camille' – my namesake – one Camille Claudel, who dominated Rodin's world and his art for nine years.

It was when Rodin and Camille Claudel were together he did his most erotic art – pairs, male and female naked, carved in stone. They were their own loving couple, she who posed for him and loved him and dwelled in his orbit as he produced his stone visions of idealized coupling.

Yet, Rodin went home every night to the Villa des Brillants, just outside Paris at Meudon, where he kept his original, peasant mistress and their illegitimate son, where he ate his cabbage soup, counted his sous, and went to bed early. Nothing Camille Claudel would ever do, no screaming scene, no threat of suicide, would shake him enough to leave his old peasant, coarse and ugly as she was.

Camille Claudel finally left Rodin in paroxysms of jealousy after nine years. He never sculpted another loving couple after she left him. She died 30 years later in a common ward, emaciated, penniless, befuddled with lost love.

I shake myself in the cold.

A man is beside me in the mist as I stand before the window of Galeries Lafayette. I have not seen him approach. I do not know from which direction he has come. I feel his presence and look up from underneath long eyelashes, to see him watching me intently, his tan raincoat outlined against the cloudlike atmosphere, trousers dark, shoes polished. He is hatless with brown, straight hair, a rough head, but I only see these things peripherally, for all I can focus on are his eyes, black-brown and piercing.

"Mademoiselle, you have an interesting face. I would like to make your portrait. I am Risto." The name means nothing to me.

I look at him shyly. All the warnings of my 17 years flash through my brain, leaving me speechless. Still, he looks decent enough and there is a compelling light in those black-brown, brown-black eyes. They are hypnotic.

After a long moment that seems separated out of time, I say slowly, "I don't speak to strangers."

I turn back to gaze absently at the new coffee machine in the store window which I have been inspecting, aware of a dynamism so strong emanating from the masculine body, I feel it reaching for me.

"I live in an apartment at number 23, rue La Boëtie," the man continues. "On the third floor, but my studio is in the same building, below street level in the back, opening onto a garden. I want to paint you. Please come there to the garden floor – and sit for me." He laughs a bit nervously.

"Oh, don't worry. I have a wife, Rose, a dancer with the Ballets Russes – and a son Roberto." He smiles enchantingly.

I am relieved. It all seems more proper to know he is married and a father. Still, the name Risto is unfamiliar but then, I know so little of art…except for Rodin, of course. I have to admit I'm flattered anyone would find me paintable.

"You seem to be so interested in the new percolator. Will you have a coffee with me? May I know your name?"

"No…no, thank you," I reply hastily, although I would have loved the warming liquid to ease the cold, and because it would be an exciting adventure to report to my friend, Suzelle. "I am Camille de St. Phalle. I live with my parents on Avenue Victor Hugo near the Bois." His smile has disappeared at my refusal to take coffee with him.

"As for being painted, I must ask their permission."

"Of course," he agrees. "Will you meet me tomorrow at this time?" It is almost 4:30 in the afternoon. "Right here…for your answer. Try to persuade them. I must paint you. I will, you know." Fleetingly, like a reflection in a pool of water, the smile, which so beguiles me, flashes through the mist and he is gone.

It seems merely a moment is over. Risto is a shadow that has vanished in a cloud, leaving me to the contemplation of a glossy coffee contraption in a shop window on a street in Paris where only a few people quickly walk by, as it is Sunday.

I know I will be here tomorrow. It will mean leaving the Lycée early. I know I must come to this place. I must see that man again.

I turn my steps to the safety of home.

I walk the whole way. He had been beside me, out of the mist, as I stood before the window of Galeries Lafayette, as if from nowhere, and just as suddenly he was gone. When the stranger had approached me and said: 'Mademoiselle, you have an interesting face. I would like to make your portrait. I am Risto,' the fog had seemed to lift, obscurity disappeared, and as if cut by the sharp lip of a prism of glass, the veiled world around me cleared.

I struggle home on wet pavements, where footprints for a moment hold. It is a lengthy walk, up the Champs-Elysée, around the Arc de Triomphe, almost to the end of Avenue Victor Hugo. The Avenue is one of the twelve spokes of the wheel that branch from the Étoile. The broad street where I live stretches southwest from the center, from the monument dedicated to the Soldat Inconnu with its living flame. I do not wish the journey to end, for the terminus home seems so mundane.

Why am I thinking of the stranger? He claims to be an artist. He is probably some hack! Perhaps he has a talent. He looked intense enough…but, to sit for a portrait? Why was I thinking all day of Rodin? Of lovers in stone? What has all this to do with Risto? Risto – a strange name that intrigues. To me, names, words, are alive with color.

I always carry a notebook and write my impressions of people, mood, the landscape, and each rendering holds something of me. After Risto had left me at Galeries Lafayette, I had brought out the little book from my string shopping bag. I pause now, on my journey homeward, under a street lamp on the corner next to Fouquet's on the Champs-Elysées. The popular bistro's outdoor terrace under its marquee, usually packed with people, is empty because of the damp chill. Through the misty air, I see the one word I had jotted upon a clean page of my notebook in large letters.

The word is RISTO and it holds the colors of the rainbow.

Finally I arrive at the wooden door of my father's house with its shining brass knocker. It is long after darkness is upon the city and the gas lights are lit, gleaming on wet streets.

Maman and Papa are waiting in the salon by a simmering fire. It has been burning for some time. They are eager for the supper Olga, our housekeeper since I was small, is fixing.

"Olga is waiting to prepare the *omelettes* – so hurry out of those damp clothes. At least take off the jacket. Here, bring it close to the fire. That's better." Maman bustles about me like a plump bumblebee, but with her, there is no sting.

Papa is reading in the wing chair by the fire, smoking a long pipe. He looks up at me quizzically.

"What took you so long? You know we always eat early on Sundays?"

"I walked home, Papa," I reply. "All the way from Galeries Lafayette."

"No wonder you're damp. Your hair is sticking to your head," he says, turning back to the papers in his lap.

"Maybe," says Maman, coming to me. "But your face is so fresh!" She has taken my face between her two hands and is turning my head from side to side, inspecting me as if looking for damage.

We enter the low-ceilinged dining room, with its bay window above the street light which sends a burnished glimmer from below. I mention nothing of my experience this day to Maman and Papa, even as they ask, in somewhat desultory manner, what adventure I have had. We consume the individual omelettes with mushrooms, a vinaigrette of grated carrot and other winter vegetables, and a runny cheese with our loaf of bread. I am ravenously hungry.

I tear the bread apart and eat so quickly I receive a reproving look from Papa, to which I exclaim, "The walk, Papa." I am monosyllabic throughout the meal, and the subject of being painted by the artist, Risto – if he really is one – seems so remote, it is stuck deep in my consciousness.

It seemed our meeting never happened.

Excusing myself early, I mount the stair-case of buffed wood to my room, and after undressing and donning a long flannel nightgown of lemon yellow, I throw myself onto the narrow bed that has been mine since I was a little girl to dream of poems and golden statues of lovers and a man's face in the mist with the darkest eyes I have ever seen.

I try to write a poem around his name, entwining the words like garlands. Perhaps because I know so little of the man, the poem 'Risto' does not materialize. I cannot seem to put down any word other than his name, and I fling the notebook to the floor in impatience, drifting into a restless sleep filled with watery dreams I cannot recollect when I awake two hours later.

The edge has been taken off my night of sleep and, picking up the notebook from the floor, I write a little verse about words I title 'The Prism', that transparent solid body dispersing and reflecting rays of light. The very last word of the poem is 'rainbow' and as I write it, Risto is alive before me. There is no more sleep this night. None at all.

Next morning, I muddle through lessons at the Lycée, unfocussed and tired. Even Suzelle notices. After lunch and the dreaded class in mathematics, I plead a headache to Madame de Champrigand, the head maitresse who, noticing my flushed face, remarks, "Go home. You may have a fever." I leave before the last class, which is music, and am back at my stand in front of Galeries Lafayette at exactly 4:30.

I find Risto awaiting me.

1927 Wintertime Paris

LE PETIT CLOS

2.

THERE IS A TINY corner of the world in Paris called Le Petit Clos – The Little Closet. Le Petit Clos, on a side alley next to rue Monsieur and across from the Musée Rodin, is a restaurant of perhaps seven tables in all, each with pink linen cloth. There is, in one corner, a wooden bar of no more than four feet in length from which the waiter (cousin of the owner) in long apron, brings aperitifs.

Madame, La Patronne, is at the cash register, next to the bar and a standing brass coat rack. The lights are dim, the food simple and unextraordinary, but early in the evening, it is virtually empty. For this reason, and for its proximity to the Lycée, the two of us find haven.

If Madame, La Patronne, recognizes her famous customer in the form of the stocky artist, she gives no sign. He is always accompanied by a girl – myself – in the blue sailor-type blouse of the Lycée uniform. The two of us sit in the far corner opposite the bar, he, over a Vermouth-Cassis and me, with a *café filtre*. Sometimes, he will order for me a *petit pain au chocolat*, a brioche roll with a piece of semi-sweet chocolate hidden in its depths, warmed to runniness. It reminds me of childhood breakfasts with hot chocolate in a cup and warm brioche. It is the only thing in these meetings that reminds me of a younger state.

We are there at least twice a week, through the long chill winter, sometimes three times. Madame observes us. The man's face, glowing from the cold outside, reflecting the pink of the linen in the soft light, seems younger than his age, and the pinkish cast to the restaurant makes me feel my face has the look of an angel. Sometimes we sit quietly for as long as an hour, barely talking, and when the first customers, locals for the most part, begin to eat their supper of white-bean cassoulet, or curried chicken legs, we take ourselves off.

Madame cannot help but notice, and far be it from her to pry – Madame is not one to pry – that my eyes rarely leave the face of my companion. They are riveted on the dynamic brown eyes, the square line of cheek and the rather Spanish look of this middle-aged Monsieur with his clay pipe. Our eyes are the only things that touch – no fingers, hands, or knees beneath the table. I will not even let him help me put on the navy blue coat of the Lycée.

It is here the wooing begins…where it is happening. I am mesmerized. I have yet to go to his studio. I have yet to pose for a portrait or to see how this man paints. I have yet to speak to my parents for permission to meet with him. At this point, I have no need to do so, successfully answering their questions so far of why I am late of an evening. It cannot go on much longer without them knowing. They are already suspicious.

But to sit with Risto, I feel an almost silent communion, like basking in a fire. When listening to his growly voice talking of art, giving me a new sight-line into its mystery, with the slight Spanish overtone to the perfect French he speaks, I am enthralled and in awe of his wisdom.

Occasionally, we stop at the Musée Rodin before it closes, on our way to Le Petit Clos, and after he has met me at the corner of rue Monsieur where he waits for me at 4:30 after my last class.

It is such a special thing to do, to go with this man to the beautiful building with its tall windows, recessed walls and enclosed garden, to walk among those sensuous loving couples in stone, to wander among them as though it were the most natural world in which to dwell, by his side, he telling me tales of the artist behind these creations. And about himself.

"I met Rodin – long ago – must have been 1912 or 13 – right here in this building – this Hôtel Biron. What a figure of a man he was! a peasant with a flowing beard. He always considered himself just a laborer – with eyes so near-sighted they had kept him from soldiering during the Franco-Prussian War. Strange for an artist of his titanic vision to have such poor sight."

Risto pauses.

"This was his studio before it became his museum. I was young then – I even tried to sculpt like he did – from clay. In fact, I copied him almost to the letter." Risto chuckles.

"You actually copied him?"

"Why not? I take from anybody – and everybody. Only I usually do it better! Many younger painters hate me to come to their exhibitions because if I see something good, I run to the studio and recreate it twice as well." He chuckles again.

We are standing before a sculpture called The Hand of God, a massive, bronze hand, held upright with two naked humans, male and female, curving and twisting, held in the palm like a ball.

"Rodin loved to do hands – twisted hands, old hands, grasping hands. One might say he was a bit tight-fisted about money – well, nothing wrong with that. I am too. Hands were important to him." Risto glances sidewise, slyly observing me. "But his greatest obsession was women...making love to them."

I gaze at the sculpture, pretending to study it, not moving a muscle as he observes me in profile.

"Three weeks before his death – in 1917 – Rodin must have been in his late 70s – one of his assistants had a life-cast make of Rodin's hand." Risto grunts. "And do you know what Rodin did? He placed a tiny torso of a naked lady in the palm!"

Risto is regarding me closely to see if I am shocked, but I steel my lips and say, "What an odd thing to do!"

"Not at all," is the reply. "Naked ladies were his favorite pastime."

I move away to look at Eternal Idol, the sculpture where a young man on his knees is bending forward to kiss the naked breast of a girl kneeling above him. The girl's hand reaches back to grasp her foot. The color rises to my cheeks because even I know the French idiom. The foot in the hand means fornication.

Risto exclaims, "The boy is lost in the blossoms." His voice is thoughtful.

"I'm hungry," I announce, and we walk quickly through the statues of the loving couples, bedded as they are in rock as if struggling to break free and soar. Each sculpture we pass of the mysteriously united figures, trembling in marble, is suddenly so alive, I find myself blushing.

"Le Petit Clos?" Risto asks.

"Of course," is my reply, and we bundle into our coats against the blustery April afternoon. If Le Petit Clos is our rendezvous, the Musée Rodin is our temple which, like an aphrodisiac, awakens the blood.

From Risto, I still keep my distance. It is becoming harder. Like a reluctant skittish female puppy, I am hard for him to leash, for I am agitated by the tentative gestures with which he has begun to touch me.

We do not reach Le Petit Clos this afternoon for constraint has a limit, and Risto's patience is wearing thin. It has been three months since first he spotted me that January Sunday, and I am conscious of a creeping anger, a hostility that seeps into his attitude toward me, making itself evident by a shortness of speech for no obvious reason, a quickness to jump on me for *naiveté* and a darkness of spirit, showing itself in silence.

On this particular April day as we make our way toward Le Petit Clos from the Musée Rodin through the eddying wind, Risto takes my tight, gloved hand in his bare one. I try to draw it away and, impatiently, he flings it aside. Marching more quickly, so it is hard for me to keep up, I call to him: "Risto, you're angry with me. Aren't we friends?"

"Sometimes I don't know!"

I stumble behind him as rapidly as I can, trying to catch up, my red scarf blowing free.

"But…but what's the matter?"

He turns to face me in the street in the middle of rue de Varenne, oblivious of passersby doing their shopping for supper at the pastry shop and greengrocer, and confronts me, stock still, hands on his hips.

"You say we're friends, but I can't even take your hand. You say we understand each other, yet you refuse to recognize me as a painter. You've shown no desire to see my work, much less realize I'm an artist who must paint you! Why, you haven't dared broach the subject – of ME – to your parents. You're afraid…too timid. I don't know why I bother with such a ninny!"

He turns and continues walking swiftly away from me.

I am stunned. I stand so long in one spot, he reaches the corner, still walking briskly. As he makes the turn, he glances back to see me running full speed toward him red scarf flying, causing several people to turn and look.

"Oh, Risto." I am breathless on reaching his side. "Forgive me. How thoughtless. Of course you are an artist, a great and famous artist, and yes, I haven't understood. It's all been so dreamlike. Please, please, don't go away!" I cannot recognize my stiff, properly-brought-up self. "I'll do anything you ask."

He looks surprised by this turn of events, by my obvious passion and excitement. "You mean that?" he asks.

"Yes."

He looks at me for a long moment.

"Well, if you mean that, then come with me, come with me right now to my studio and at least look at my work. Perhaps you'll find it as beautiful as Rodin's. One never knows. But in any case, it'll be a beginning to understanding me, a beginning to our beginning. Then I want you to go home and speak to your parents about letting me paint you…tonight you speak to them! You understand? Tonight!"

And grabbing my gloved hand, he pulls me after him, both of us still distraught, at a rapid pace.

I am bodily dragged to the studio,

Without a protest.

1927 Early April Paris

THE STUDIO

3.

This is the way I come to his studio on the ground floor of a building on rue La Boëtie, opening onto a tangled garden. The room smells of paint and clay and turpentine. It is laden with pictures, stacked on the floor or hanging, to almost completely cover all four walls of the large room, save for a cracked mirror over one of the tables and a pair of glass doors to the garden. A gas grill and ice chest are in the corner near the entry door.

It is a turbulent place with a couch covered in flowered cloth, and two wooden tables with paint pots and brushes. The whole room blazes color, as Risto lights a gas lamp and two large candles. The light flickers over some of the African shapes and incomprehensible abstracts in eerie fashion, as in some pagan temple, and Risto's shadow, enlarged by the light behind him, looms portentously on one wall.

"Oh," is all I can breathe. It is spectacular, frightening, all at the same time. I enter the room as I tentatively see, with relief, Risto lighting the coal in a small grate, for I am trembling, perhaps from the cold of early evening.

As the room begins to warm, he roughly pulls open the door of a low cabinet and brings forth a half-full bottle of wine, a raw, peasant red wine, his favorite I was to learn, and two glass goblets. I stand awkwardly in the middle of the room, feeling thrust into an alien world.

I watch as he pours the burgundy. He sloshes it carelessly. Is he still so upset with me? I came here, didn't I? Isn't that what he wished?

"Sit down," he says without ceremony, peeling off his coat as he nods to the couch against the wall opposite the thicket garden beyond the French doors. I remove my coat and gloves and sit on the edge of the couch, coat on the floor, neatly folded, gloves on top.

Handing me a glass of wine, taking the other in his large hand, he throws himself down beside me so strongly, drops splash onto my blue skirt. How to explain that to Maman! I dab futilely at the stain with my scarf.

"See that cracked mirror over there?" he asks, a non sequitor if ever there was one! "Self portraits…I do a lot of them…sometimes even leave in the crack! Got really angry one day – and poof." He flicks the wine cork at the mirror and lights his clay pipe with angry puffs of smoke. I can see the embers glow red.

Is he trying to frighten me?

"Self-portraits! Must be my big ego. Well, Rembrandt did a lot of them. Rembrandt went bankrupt, you know, and his creditors auctioned off all the possessions left to him by his rich wife who died young, except for a mirror which enabled him to paint himself, which he did over and over again."

Then, suddenly, "I'm sure this must interest my little art student, eh? Isn't that why you bother with me at all?" he says with a hint of disgust.

There is silence, save the hissing from the grate. The candles flicker and glow, and I continue to dab my wine spot absently.

"Will you stop that," he snaps, flinging himself off the couch abruptly, going to the glass garden doors and gazing out into the blackness.

"Oh, Risto"…I murmur.

Again silence.

Then bitterly, "Not that you care, but do you know how I got the name Risto? From Fragonard, of all people. He was a court painter in the 18th century, famous for his pictures of Venuses in various stages of undress. He did a picture called The Girl on a Swing…some courtier or other's mistress…with her legs in the air, her ruffled skirts tossing.

Below her in the garden, is her lover, half lying in the grass with his eyes popping, you see, "Risto turns to face me, brown eyes glistening, "underpants hadn't yet been invented."

I feel myself turn purple.

Risto returns to glaring out the glass doors. There is silence again, hissing silence.

"He always signed his paintings 'Frago'-just 'Frago'-to hell with Fragonard," he says savagely. "I like Risto a lot better than Ruy Aristide, don't you? RISTO," he repeats, rolling the R with a wave of his hand and a snap of the fingers in a Spanish gesture. "RISTO," he says once more, emphasizing the IST." Very artISTic, don't you think? Or maybe irresISTible."

Hiss, the silence seems to echo.

"Mireilles gave me the nickname...my older sister Mireilles." He pauses. "She died of tuberculosis at 15. Ah, she was good to me, always stealing extra sweets for me. Being so much younger than the others, I was never strong enough to grab my share." Risto sips his wine thoughtfully. His pipe has gone out. "She used to come to my room at night, make sure I was covered like a little mother." Risto's voice has softened. Then, "But what do you care?"

I am mute.

"You don't care, do you Camille?" he says, turning to come and stand before me, almost humbly. "Risto has just been an amusing way for you to pass the time, for you to see Rodin in a new light and eat your *petit pain au chocolat*, like a little girl."

In the studio by the hissing grate and flickering candles, we gaze deeply at each other, eyes locked.

"I'm miserable, " Risto suddenly says, his voice grating, as he puts his pipe on the table and sits beside me, settling back against the cushions of the couch. His face is brooding, the dark eyes flecked with reddish specks. I can hear the liquid plunk of drops from the gutter in regular beat.

"I always thought a studio would be high up in a loft," I say finally.

"Not necessarily," he says as if just awakened. "The light here pours through the double doors. There are few high buildings across from me, and sometimes I move out, easel and all, and work right in the tangle of the garden. This is my castle. Nobody bothers me here." His voice drifts off.

"Camille!"

Suddenly he sits up, and setting down both our glasses upon the floor, he grasps my hands, which curl like dry leaves in his own. He turns them over, looking closely at them, spreading the fingers apart, one by one, and unexpectedly bending his head, places his lips in the center of one of my palms. I am gazing down at the silky, brown hair at the nape of his neck. His lips are impersonal, like the skin of a cool orange.

Raising his head, he silently lifts my right hand and places the palm against his cheek, slightly scratchy to the touch and infinitely warm. His face appears large. I can see every pore of the skin, a brown freckle on his left brow, a small nick on his chin. The eyes, red and gold now, are imploring.

"Cammy, you're crying," he says with astonishment. My eyes feel full of tears, through which his face is reflected as through two round prisms.

Drawing me to him, he exclaims, "My darling little girl, you're not angry with me? Forgive me, Cammy."

"No." I pull away from him.

"Say something. Please talk to me."

I recover myself. The tears are swallowed up, leaving behind a stinging sensation in eyes and throat.

I sit closer to him on the flowered couch, not quite sure why. I urgently want the shelter of his shadow. I do not wish to ignite him, neither his anger, nor a sentimental approach, but I feel the need of him. My hands, stiff sticks a moment ago, lie soft in his. My head is upon his shoulder, a tentative trial he accepts. He holds me gently. Then abruptly, sitting forward, facing me round to him, so we are almost comically nose-to-nose, he smiles that entrancing smile.

"Do you think there will ever be a point when you will let me love you?"

"Well," I begin lamely, "I know you have a certain affection for me. Why else would you put up with me?" I find myself sounding coquettish. "You know how I look forward to our meetings near the Lycée – our Petit Clos – to the hot chocolate in the rain – what you've taught me. Such a wonderful friend."

"Friend!" He jumps to his feet. "You don't know what you're saying, by half!" His eyes are staring at the floor. My friendship is not what he seeks!

"It's been months! How much patience must a man have! And in more months time, I expect it will be the same little Camille whose eyes look at me from their corners and a mouth like stone."

"Risto, come sit with me. Sit here." The voice with which I speak holds a summons I do not recognize.

Risto comes and sits beside me on the couch, which bounces disconcertingly. I lift my head accepting the inevitable, surely a kiss. He merely holds me. With a sigh, he draws me closer to him and I see, bending gently toward me, the solemn face of a mature man I do not even know, the face of a stranger.

Our faces almost touch. I am breathless, struggling a little against his chest, my neck curving back like a bow. It is at this precise instant, Risto's lips touch my own.

My eyes are wide open, trying to dazzle those dark eyes above me.

The mouth which kisses me is not flaming. It is sweet, with a gentle force, increasing in weight upon me, until my lips with no will of their own, separate, as predictably as an orange breaks apart and opens under pressure.

I press close to his chest. Finally, confident I am not going to pull away, he moves from me and gazes at me. I wonder, lazily, if he plans to remove my clothes here and now and make love to me. His look is one of sensuous expectation.

All I can do is breathe, "Please kiss me." He complies eagerly, and I bathe in a witless unaccountability. He gathers me in his arms as though I am a bunch of limp waterlilies.

I cease to belong to myself. My hand, resting on his thigh, which flesh seems to burn through the trouser cloth, no longer belongs to the body from which it came.

All I can envision is Rodin's The Kiss, the lady of that couple. I am a Rodin human, quivering in the marble. Only my body is not of marble. It feels boneless, melting, like syrup.

We rest. I manage to stand beside the couch and, floating with outstretched arms, I go to the cracked mirror on the wall, his self-portrait mirror, to see my metamorphosis. My features, in the flickering candlelight, look newly roused from sleep, lips trembling. They are my lips, aren't they? I see a new person, a person of recent origin, newly minted only arrived lately at 23, rue la Boëtie and ready to remain forever.

Risto rises from the couch and moving in back of me puts his arms around my waist from behind. He too gazes into the mirror, cheek against mine, and although the crack in it seems to split us apart, our faces are coupled together. He even looks like me!

"My darling little girl. Only yesterday – you were like a pup, ready to bolt. Now you seem ready to be collared, tethered and led? Am I right, Cammy?" and he tosses his head back and laughs.

I am so startled, I laugh too.

He is right. I am not only ready to be collared, tethered and led, but eager to be pampered and patted, ready to sit eagerly at his feet... and all that that implies.

HOME

4.

"RISTO IS A BASTARD!" shouts my father. Papa never swears. Papa never shouts. "He's a charlatan! Do you know he's married? Huh! That doesn't stop him as far as women are concerned. He's notorious!"

"Please, Gerard, not in front of the child," interjects Maman.

I am numb. I had left Risto's studio, knees weak, after managing to keep him at arm's length, promising to speak that evening to my parents about a portrait. We did not even kiss goodbye.

I had made up my mind. I walked across Paris, panting a bit from the steam rising from the pavements, the lights reflected in their blackish surfaces, treading the blurred avenues, above which seemed to appear a face, rising and whispering 'Stay'. I walked in bursts of energy, filled with a mixture of joy and qualms and a guilt I believed I was supposed to feel, knowing already which route I would take – with Risto – not the dutiful, daughterly route – but the other – the route of love.

I hear my father's voice swirling about me, and Maman repeating over and over: "But he is a Spaniard. One must be so careful with the Spanish," as if his nationality were a dirty word.

My father is going on about one young model with whom Risto lived for a month, and of whom he painted 40 enormous oils.

"Imagine! That's more than one a day! The woman must have stayed naked the entire time!" Papa explodes.

"Gerard, please."

"No, really, Camille. This is not to be tolerated…for you to consider being painted by such a…and at your age. Not to be tolerated!" My father is facing me squarely.

"He needs women…'to fuel his talent', he says. Indeed! What an outrageous excuse for being a libertine. 'Through sex, I reach some essence', he says. Huh. Why, It's almost as though he paints with his…"

"Gerard!"

"Do you know, young lady, his father threw him out? The older man was a painter in Barcelona, and a good one, I'm told. He was so enraged at finding that…that presumptuous Risto doctoring one of his own father's paintings, he threw brushes and palette and colors at him spattering him from head to toe. Humph, he must have looked a splotchy mess, a blasted rainbow. Then…out!"

A rainbow! The colors swim before my eyes.

My father has paused to catch his breath, but I can see from his face, inside he is still sputtering.

"And you want to be painted by that man?"

"Yes."

"No, young lady. That's final!"

There is a short pause in which we eye each other, before he is off again.

"Are you so easily flattered by this lecherous creature? And he's old…must be 45, if he's a day."

"Papa, you exaggerate!"

"I don't! This is unthinkable, Camille. You should not even be a 'friend' of this man, much less be looking at his pictures. Has he shown them to you?"

"Well," I answer in a subdued voice. "I've seen one or two, stacked against the wall…or hanging on it. I didn't really look too closely…"

"And just where did you see his paintings 'stacked against the wall or hanging on it?'" He is imitating my voice in quite an insulting fashion.

I am silent, eyes downcast, ominously calm.

"Exactly where, Miss?"

"At his studio on rue La Boëtie," I reply.

"At his studio! Do you hear that, Giselle? Now you understand why your daughter is often late…where she is spending her after-school hours and with whom!" My father is pacing rapidly back and forth on the Aubusson carpet, one of our family's most prized possessions. My lowered eyes trace the design, with its orange and peacock blue figuration. I had never before noticed how beautiful it is.

"Risto, Risto, indeed! Do you know, my young lady, he never paints men, only women. Sometimes there's a bull standing in for a man, but he is obsessed with women. And they are ugly, ugly pictures. Why, oh why, would you want to be painted by that man…in that way?"

"Papa, he wouldn't paint me that way." I raise my eyes to his.

My father regards me seriously for a long moment, as if seeing me anew. "Just how far has this gone?" he says, in a low tone. "Are you his latest obsession?"

"It hasn't 'gone' anywhere at all."

"Well, it shall go no further, I can assure you. This is all too ridiculous."

"Papa, it's not ridiculous. It's the most serious thing in my life."

"Enough," he interjects.

"Not enough," I say with anger. "You don't understand. Risto is the most exciting person I ever met. He teaches me…"

"Enough," my father roars. Maman is weeping, huddled in the big wing chair by the fireplace. The fireplace is cold. After a long look, I turn and leave the graceful living room going into the foyer and out the polished wooden door with its brass knocker on the outside that shines in the streetlight.

It's done! I have told them all there is to tell…well, almost all. What a relief. It is a sweet feeling to be relieved by the truth (not about our kisses…never that). Three and one-half months of secrets, of concealment, have been a burden. The excuses I have contrived for my parents have cost energy. But the deepest drain by far has been the pack of plausible explanations I have given myself.

I have received the sudden, cold dampening of spirit I anticipated. Suddenly, weary no more, I am in haste, driven. I run quickly, shaking myself, and even though the streets of Paris are damp and dark, they burst with April promise. I remove my hat, and holding it in one hand, the moist air clean in my hair, I run over the cobblestones. I run to him.

I do not find the reply I expect. The studio is empty. I have run across half of Paris on this April earlynight, impelled by a force beyond my control. I anticipate a passionate embrace in the warm room with the grate hissing and the candles flickering. Tonight is not the night.

I tap futilely on the studio door, having descended the steps below street level leading to it. I do not dare to call too loudly, arousing the sleepy concierge in her glass cage-like room by the main door, and, worse, of attracting the family on the third floor.

The family! It is the first time I have thought of Risto and Rose and Roberto in this way. The family! What a terrible word. Like Maman, Papa and myself! Would Rose be preparing the evening meal for the threesome, before leaving for the ballet? Would there be a hissing grate upstairs beside which they would warm themselves? Would the child cry? How old is he? Does he have the magnificent, dark eyes of his father? Would Risto kiss Rose goodbye? And where will he go if she does have a dancing engagement? Will he stay and mind the child?

These questions swirl through my head as if on gusts of wind, questions I have never permitted myself to ask before. There, pressed next to the door of his empty studio, imagining the warmth on the third floor above me, I feel desolate.

Can his kiss change my life so much?

I feel like a bird caught between two nests, the one, my home with a waiting mother and angry father, disapproving and sour about my association with Risto; the other, the nest I am driven and determined to build with him.

Bedraggled, chilled to my most inner reaches, not only by the wind and damp streets, but more profoundly by the thought of the domestic scene on the third floor above, I quietly turn and make my way, all eagerness gone, to the heavy oak door of my father's house with its brass knocker on the Avenue Victor Hugo near the Bois.

As I had forgotten my key in my haste, I am forced to knock. This simple action seems to harden the resolve inside me.

Olga, the Russian-born housekeeper, lets me in, whispering my parents are at the table in the dining room. Scented with garlic and lemons from the kitchen, Olga is comfortable and kind. I have the feeling she thinks my father too hard on me. It is unspoken, of course, but she is gentleness itself, as I thank her for letting me in. I remove my coat, smooth the uniform skirt with its fading wine stains and slowly approach the dining room.

There is silence, a silence as dark as the stains on my skirt. There is nothing but the click of fork and knife. They know I am home. They would have heard the knocker.

Home is suddenly an unfamiliar place. It seems to have shrunk. The big clock in the hall, the polished rosewood table against the foyer wall, even the smell of the leg of lamb – things from which I always draw comfort – ease my anxiety not at all this night. It is a disorienting sensation, as if I am already elsewhere.

I enter the room, which is brightly lit, revealing my frozen state and seat myself at my place at the table. Not a word is spoken. There is only the sound of munching, eating sounds and clinks. Maman in her printed challis dress, Papa in his severe gray suit, neither gives a glance in my direction.

I eat little.

Finally, Papa pushes back in his chair, wipes his mouth with the linen napkin, and faces me squarely.

"This is unconscionable behavior. To flit off into the night like some… moth. I'll not permit it again."

He pauses. Then, his curiosity showing, "Did you see your precious artist? Did he greet you with open arms? Or did you run into his wife? Heh?"

I feel my mouth trembling and my eyes fill.

"My God, Camille, this man is only a dauber of paint…He's a libertine! A womanizer! And you're not yet 18 years old!" Throwing the napkin down, rising brusquely to his feet, Papa says in a loud voice, "No more. Never again!" Then, after turning to my mother, "Giselle, talk some sense into her," he quickly leaves the room.

The tears are rolling down my cheeks. I make no sound. I feel separated out, my new goodbye to the old.

My mother clears her throat, sensing the intensity of my dilemma. She always appears so calm to me, but not tonight. She fidgets with the lace handkerchief she habitually carries. She is not a pouncer like Papa. She permits me to recover my composure and dab away the tears with my napkin.

"My dear child. How can this be so serious to you, that you would run out in the middle of the night after some…artist…and against your father's wishes? And you know your father. Anyone who is not practical, he disdains. You know what a functionalist he is."

After waiting a few moments for a response, she finally says, again showing the perplexity and curiosity both my parents share: "Well… did you see him?"

"The studio was locked."

"How long have you known this man and, for heaven's sake, how did you manage to meet him?"

"He introduced himself to me one afternoon, in front of the big department store, the Galeries Lafayette. I was looking in the window and he asked to paint me. That's all there was to it."

"He approached you on the street? You permitted this? Camille, I'm shocked. Why it's enough to notify the police!"

"Oh, Maman! No…" I am genuinely alarmed. "He wasn't bold with me. He didn't suggest anything improper. He never has." (Oh, lies, lies. It has been in his every gesture). "He explained he was married and had a son in the first sentence, the first time we met."

"And what does that mean?" replies my mother. "Just when did this 'meeting' take place? Have you seen him since many times?"

"Early this winter."

"How early?"

"In January."

"You mean you've seen him all through this winter…since January?" Maman is aghast.

I can hear the clock ticking all the way from the hall. Maman's handkerchief has become a ball.

"How frequently do you meet? And," she colors slightly, "and just what do you do? Camille, I expect answers…truthful ones."

"Well, we meet for coffee at a small place near the Lycée…he has taken me to the Musée Rodin…"

"Not Rodin too…He has a worse reputation than Risto…"

"Maman, Rodin is dead!"

"I know, but some of his sculptures are hardly what a young girl should be looking at. Don't tell your father!" The balled handkerchief is now the size of a large grape. "And his studio? Risto's, I mean, how often have you been there?"

"This afternoon was the only time, I swear it."

Maman looks me full in the eyes. "At least that's one thing. She reaches for my hand. "And, of course, it will be the last time you ever go there. This must be understood. And never again must you meet with him after school for coffee or Rodin or anything else.

"You don't know what you ask!" I feel the blood leave my face.

"He is a disreputable man…"

I look at my mother blankly.

"Do you understand what I'm saying?"

I nod.

"Then, it's agreed?"

I nod again.

"No, I want to hear your promise…that you will not see him again."

Choking on the words, an almost inaudible "I promise" emits, of itself, from my lips. Rising to her feet, handkerchief now so small as to be invisible in her hand, my mother kisses me on the brow and leaves the room with a swish of her challis skirt.

I make my way with shaky steps to my room with its narrow, child's bed. I am gray with the knowledge that now I must go underground. Now deception begins in earnest. The lies will mount burying the past, with all its filial devotion, the other springs, summers autumns, winters, which passed all too swiftly, leaving only the gentle memories of Maman…Papa. Maman. I bitterly cry myself to sleep, this night, on the hard pillow, each acid tear announcing that every good and beautiful thing must come to an end…sometime.

1927 Springtime Paris

TEETER-TOTTER

5.

IT IS A SPRING filled with soft days of tulips and purple irises, white arum lilies and red roses. The gardens of the Bois are incredibly lovely. The scent in the streets is enough to lull my self-doubt as I make my way across Paris. Like a child's pull-toy! I wonder if the end of the string is at rue La Boëtie, or is it at Avenue Victor Hugo?

It is an uncomfortable spring. My lies are constant to the point I am as glib and slippery as a piece of soap.

Suzelle, always loyal, is corroborating my stories, intrigued by what she calls 'Camille's Adventure with a capital A'. Suzelle, with the little, pointed teeth of a ferret, and sparkling eyes, knows. She knows everything…almost.

"You've got to be careful, Camille," she squeals at me, one superb day in May, at school. "Your father must be getting really suspicious."

She is right! He has taken to meeting me at 4:20 every afternoon and unceremoniously escorting me home, only to return to his office for another two hours of work. Our journeys together are conducted in virtual silence.

Maman is not usually home before 6:30 from an afternoon of cards or from working at her thrift shop, of which she is President. Gentle, apprehensive Maman, managing a large body of middle-aged ladies!

The gap in time gives me the chance to escape, after pleading a school errand with Olga.

Often, I streak to Risto's studio for an hour, or sometimes to Le Petit Clos, back across town from which I have just come.

"Such a waste of time," I say to Suzelle. "Papa should really check with Maman, don't you think? I wonder why he hasn't. My good luck, I guess." Secretly, I feel he does not want to discover the truth. However, I am always sure to be home before his return.

And Risto...Risto of the open arms! So great is the pull to his studio, I seem to have no will in the matter. Oh, he has me well in hand with his kisses! They are enough to make me reel.

I am technically a virgin still. I marvel at Risto's control. How does he manage to break away from me at the crucial moment? Is it because he runs home to a marital partner? Or another lover?

The thought makes my stomach turn over. Is it perhaps because I am under age? It seems a silly thought as I will be 18 so soon...in July.

When the kissing ends, after increasingly extended encounters, I am left wanting and angry. "Why not, Risto?" I say, to which he replies, "The time is not yet ripe." How can he resist?

He soothes my rumpled ego, makes hot chocolate, mixed with egg so it froths in the cup, or we share red wine and cheese, or new strawberries, dipped in sugar.

Home on the Avenue Victor Hugo with its oak door and brass knocker, symbolizing all that is cold and lifeless, is now only a fixed point from which I run, returning before my parents, these balmy spring evenings. I feel like a rubber band, stretched and taut. One day I know it will snap.

The day it does is a horror. It is a misty, late May evening, colder than normal for the season. I return to Avenue Victor Hugo on the autobus, aware I am later than usual but still in time for my self-imposed deadline. Dismounting the bus, I scatter a multitude of blackbirds, which toss off angrily in all directions. A fore-boding of ill? I race nervously up the broad avenue of my home and fling myself at the massive door. Papa has taken away my key.

After a moment knocking, Olga admits me, her stolid face somber and with a finger to her lips, points at the salon. With a shake of her head, exuding her characteristic garlicky smell, she pads back to the kitchen. I see Papa's gray hat on the rosewood table by the front door.

Smoothing my navy blue skirt, holding head erect to give the illusion of a confidence I do not feel, I enter the salon to see Papa with his back to me, staring at the empty, unlit fireplace. Maman with her lawn handkerchief clutched in hand sits in the wing chair beside it.

There is a strange flavor to their attitudes.

"I'm finally home after a dreadful bus ride," I say in my gayest voice. "It was so crowded! Don't know what's happening these days. There seem to be so many more people." I throw myself onto the loveseat opposite Maman.

There is no response to this small outburst. Maman's round blue eyes don't meet mine but are fixed on the floor.

The minutes tick.

"And poor Suzelle. She's really going to catch it. She was supposed to be home at 6:15...her aunt is coming to dinner all the way from Brittany, especially to see her. And here it is, very nearly 7:00 o'clock. You know how strict her parents are. They never..."

"Camille stop lying!" My father's voice cuts through the aimless chatter. I freeze.

"What?" I manage to retort. I only trust my voice to the briefest response because I can hear my heart beating there.

"I said stop lying."

"I don't know what you mean."

"You know exactly what I mean," Papa says, turning to face the room. His eyes meet mine and bore into me as sharply as the dentist's pick.

"Why do you assume I lie?" I say in my haughtiest tones.

"Oh, that's easy," he says, his sarcasm pouring over me like oil. "First it has become a habit of yours, and second, your little yarn about good old Suzelle just doesn't hold up."

"But we had been shopping and the time just sped by."

"Stop it. Don't make it any worse!"

There is a mighty pause, Papa and I trying to stare each other down. I do not waver. Neither does he.

Slowly, he stands with hands clasped behind his back, he devastatingly proceeds to explain my lie.

"Your silly friend, Suzelle, stopped by here about 5:30. I happened to have returned for some papers and decided it not necessary to rush back to the office again this evening. There was this great banging on the door. I opened it and Suzelle burst through nearly knocking me over...let her in myself, I did. She turned brick pink and said 'My God, you're home!' in such a loud voice, it was almost a shout. Now, just why should it be so surprising to find a man home at 5:30 in the evening?"

Damn Suzelle! Why did she have to come blundering in here.

"Camille, I demand an explanation."

"Well, I certainly don't know why Suzelle was here. I had just seen her, for heaven's sake."

"You know that is not the question I am asking." There is a long pause. "Just where were you?"

I give a deep sigh. I know when I am defeated and find it difficult to prevaricate further.

"If you want to know what I really think," I begin feebly.

"I do NOT want to know what you really think," Papa says harshly. "I want to know where you were and with whom."

Tick, tick from the standing clock in the hall. Maman's face is turned from me. She is pale.

"You were with him, weren't you, that artist fellow, that Risto! And no more lies, Camille."

The rubber band is snapping.

"Yes, I was."

Papa gives a loud, martyr's sigh.

"Are you such a child that you'll have to have a maid to watch you – Olga, for instance – to escort you everywhere? Is this what you're asking for?"

Maman speaks up for the first time and her words stab me.

"You promised me, Camille," she says sadly. Tears prick my eyes.

"You were at his studio?" Papa continues.

"Yes."

"And just what did you and your lover do?"

"He is not my lover."

"I wish I could believe that."

"Why can't you? It's true."

"Because I no longer trust you."

"He made me hot chocolate," I manage to mumble.

"Hot chocolate! How charming! Risto making hot chocolate!"

"You don't need to make it sound stupid."

"Camille," Maman gasps.

"Well, all this ridicule, Maman. Neither of you have ever taken me seriously."

"If you mean we've never taken your liaison seriously, you must be out of your head. It is because we do take it seriously, these scenes disrupt our lives, ruin our days and give us sleepless night," Papa says.

"I'm sorry for that."

"And after the hot chocolate?"

"After?"

"Yes. What else did you do there?"

"Oh, not much…looked at some pictures."

Papa turns again to the empty fireplace, its brass andirons shining too brightly on the cold hearth. His hands are still clasped behind his back.

"What do you suggest we do?" His voice is resigned. Is he trying to be diplomatic?

"Why don't you do nothing."

"Nothing, you say?" He is all heat again. "While my daughter is being seduced by this dissolute, middle-aged…"

"He's a great man."

"My God!"

"Papa," I say, rising. Maybe standing will give me new energy. "I'm old enough to choose my own friends. I'll be 18 in July. I have a mind of my own. I should be trusted to have some judgement."

"Friends? Judgement? Trust? You're making a joke!" Papa turns to me. His watch chain gleams malevolently in the lamplight. Though not a big man, he is far bigger than I, trim and straight and vested and steely cold, with pale eyes piercing to my depths.

"Let's take that one by one. Risto, a friend? Don't be absurd. He wants only one thing, the thing he is most famous for – and that is not his pictures!" He says this with a roar. "By going to his studio, you are labeled – for all the world to see. You are one of Risto's whores!" He is red with anger and I am pale with guilt, and a whisper of something else. A Risto whore?

"As for judgement, what possible good judgement can be observed in a young 'supposed' lady going to the rooms of a libertine. Think of the neighbors. They are certainly going to wonder how the devil your mother came up with a child like you, with the morals of a street girl."

Maman winces.

"And that, by God, reflects on me! And as for trust, young lady," he continues. It is now my turn to wince. "You have not earned it with your interminable lies. You lie as easily as a little serpent, these days, Camille."

"Oh Papa," I sigh.

"Is this to be the way you live your life? One of deception of all who believe in you? I can't say that I do anymore. Your mother and I," – Maman's face is shrouded in melancholy – "have been proud of you. We have been pleased with your lessons, your manners – up until now. But we see danger for you with this Risto man. More important, we are disgusted with the lying that takes you away from us...takes you away from yourself. Trust? Hah!"

I am shaking.

"Alright," I blurt. "I am not worthy of your trust. I've been deceiving you all along. I see Risto as often as he can arrange. Papa, Maman," I turn from one to the other with supplicating hands. "You've forced me to lie. You don't recognize the fact I have feelings of my own. You treat me like a little girl – with my pleasing manners – whatever they may be. You have been judging me too closely...or maybe from too far away." My words come out in spurts.

"Camille!" my father exclaims.

"It's not a fair judgement. I have been seeing Risto. He lights my life...he teaches my things...he is strong and caring and creative. Oh, not perfect, of course. He's pretty messy," I say feebly.

"Messy!" Papa interjects. "If you mean his personal life, you have a point. Have you met his wife yet? How about his son, eh? Just where do you fit into this homey picture, my girl? Just where do you visualize yourself in this family?" The last word is a shout.

"Family?" I shout back. "I hate 'family,' certainly if this is any example."

"Camille," Maman cries gently.

"I don't care about family...his or ours! I care about Risto! Whatever my place in his life, I accept it with joy because I believe in him – in his talent and in his feelings for me. By the way, Papa, nothing," and again I shout, "nothing has HAPPENED between us that would make me a whore, one of his many whores you presume to exist. We've done nothing wrong – and to hell with the neighbors. If I don't care, why should you?" I am breathing hard.

Maman is on her feet, approaching me as if I am a snapping dog.

"Camille, I have never seen you like this. I don't understand. We've done nothing but care for you. Maybe we've spoiled you. You're so willful. I don't recognize you."

Suddenly, I cruelly speak out the truth.

"I know what I want. I know what I must have. I'll live here with you, if you'll permit it. It will be an armed truce," I say, with a dry laugh, "but at least you'll have the satisfaction of knowing where I sleep at night. Your reputation will suffer less than if you throw me out. For if you throw me out, you and I know exactly where I'll go and with whom I'll be!"

As Papa rushes from the room, I feel the angry whoosh of air physically hitting me as he passes. He has interrupted me in midsentence, I think resentfully. He has heard nothing I have been saying. Or maybe he has heard it all.

In front of me stands Maman. We are the same size, the same coloring, only Maman's figure is more billowy than my own. There, in her burgundy colored dress with light blue flowers, a dress I will never forget, she regards me balefully for a long moment.

My eyes do not waver from hers.

With a deep sigh, she says, "Have you any idea what this is doing to your father?"

"I know, Maman," I reply humbly.

"Do you? I wonder. My dear and only child, is there nothing I can say to you?"

"No, Maman."

"Well," she says, looking at the ceiling, then back to me, "I guess your father and I have lost the battle. May God bless you, and Camille, watch for promises. You take your own too lightly. Someday, someone else may do the same."

Promises! How I have broken mine to Maman! I have lied so outrageously, I no longer recognize this self, this me. Ah, promises! At least Risto has made me none. There is no vow to break. The electric bond between us needs none. It is just there, to be tested and played out. It is life itself.

Oh, Maman. Oh, Papa. What am I doing to you? I am destroying your world, in which I was an integral part, even the focus. I am destroying it as easily as lighting a match to tinder in the hearth.

I sit crumpled in the chair for a long time. There is no dinner. There are no words. There is nothing.

Maman and Papa have lost the battle. They have lost the war. What a bitter victory for me. Above all, they have lost the peace.

For now, we live the next weeks in semi-silence. There is no real communication between us, only a veiled hostility, although sometimes I catch Maman watching me in unguarded moments with such a sad expression she breaks my heart. They do not have the stomach to throw me out. So, added to my deceit, I now have the guilt of exploiting their good intentions and the kindness of their parenthood. Deceiver, exploiter. What a pretty creature am I!

The rubber band has snapped.

STILL LIFE

6.

THE GLASS DOORS OF the studio at 23, rue La Boëtie are open to the garden, on this balmy June day. I am going to be painted! Finally, my portrait will be produced. It has been almost six months from the day a stranger approached me in the cold mist in front of the Galeries Lafayette.

It is close to 11:00 o'clock in the morning. I sit upon the flowered couch, sipping a *café filtre* Risto has prepared, watching as he sets up the easel and lays out pots and tubes of color on the two stained, wooden tables. Cleaning his brushes, he chatters happily about – of all people, Modigliani.

"What a painter! He was supremely gifted, though I wasn't that aware of the fact while he was living. He gave me one of his paintings, and one day needing canvas, I painted it over. This picture would be very valuable today. I've been kicking myself ever since."

Risto proceeds to hoist a huge six-foot by four-foot blank canvas onto the easel, facing tall. I am astonished by its size.

"That…that's not for my portrait, is it," I exclaim. "My face will be…enormous!"

"Of course it is, my love – and who says I'm just going to paint your face!"

He is struggling with the canvas still, facing it toward him, with his back to the glass doors where the light flows in. All I can see are the struts of the back of the easel and his legs and feet beneath.

"Modigliani's portraits were never 'slices of life', you know," Risto chatters from behind the canvas. "He penetrated the personality. Poor drunk! Died at the age of 36 of consumption…and drugs, liquor…"

"How could he be such a fine painter if he drank so much?"

"He just was." Risto pops out his head. "He used to get so drunk, he'd dance naked in the street with only a scarf around his waist, pretending to be a bull-fighter." Risto laughs and goes behind the easel. "In a bistro one night, he was making drawings of the patrons and got so depressed, he took the drawings into the latrine and pinned them on the spike…as toilet paper! I was there." I hear Risto fussing with his pots of paint, sloshing turpentine into a metal cup.

"Then, you know what he did. He dragged his girl friend…"

"Was he married?"

"No…his *petite amie*…forget her name, but a mousey little thing. They had a baby, if I remember right…anyway he dragged her out of the café and through the streets by the hair. Yet," Risto says, suddenly appearing again from behind the canvas, "his nudes are among the most beautiful in the world. Your portrait will be quite different. I don't want you to expect to look like one of his."

"Why would I? You're not he. I'm sure you're a much better painter. Besides, I've never seen a Modigliani."

"I'm glad for your confidence, and now, Mademoiselle, it is your turn." He comes to me.

"What do you mean, 'my turn'?"

"First I must kiss you…and then get down to work." We do not 'get down to work' for some time.

Our kisses over the past weeks have increased in fervor. Risto has developed the ritual of caressing me and stroking the length of my hip that stretches away from him.

This time, there is a difference. I do not stay the hands, which play upon my body. I know I am about to succumb to a most frightening joy. I envision our two bodies joined together like the two halves of a single beast.

Holding me to him, he looks down in my face and says most seriously, and to my surprise: "How old are you, Cammy?"

"I don't ask you any questions," I reply.

Risto is surprised.

"Oh, come now," I continue. I'll be 18 the 12th of July, and do try to remember it."

"Then it's time, the age of consent."

"Time for what?" I say with contrived *naiveté.*

"Time for you to sit for me."

"I'm ready for anything you want."

He rises from the divan, and going to the easel, picking up the largest brush, says, "Well, let's start then."

"Now?" I say, with a little cry. My vision of the coupled beast has not happened. I am left hungry. "Why do you stop now?"

Why do these loving sessions always leave me more upset than he? Can it be because there is always Rose, to whom he can run afterwards? Rose is there for him to make love to freely, peremptorily, having been aroused by the lush body I possess, a sickening thought.

I am not prepared for what follows. After making some quick movements on the canvas, which I can hear rather than see, he puts down the brush and comes over to me.

"I want you to lie back like this among the cushions," he says, fixing me in the position he wants, one leg stretched out, the other slightly curled under me. I feel languid as a rag doll.

"And let's get rid of all these clothes?"

At this, he starts to undress me. I am oblivious to any sense of embarrassment.

He slides the checkered skirt from beneath me, pulls off the under drawers, removes my blouse, already unbuttoned, takes off my chemise. I am naked, lolling there like a sleek cat.

"You're beautiful," he says, in a voice so thick, it is hard to recognize, and he gazes at me so somberly and for so long a time, I wonder if something is wrong. But he does not touch me again.

Then, going quickly to the easel, he disappears and knowing he can see me nude and exposed while he is dressed and most often concealed by the canvas, I suddenly blush.

It is all very strange. At first, silence. Then I hear him utter low cries. He pants. He heaves. He emerges briefly, from time to time, his face flushed. At one point, I am almost afraid the huge canvas will be knocked over. This goes on for more than two hours.

Finally, throwing down the brush with a loud, "Done!" he is upon me, stripping his clothes so quickly I do not even see him remove them. We are both consumed. I hold him tight between my knees, transported to some exquisite plateau behind my shuttered lids. Our lovemaking is a battle we both win. I plunge from the top to the bottom of some deep and wide chasm. The double-backed beast has conquered.

If there was ever a doubt in my mind, it is stilled forever by the imperious savagery of this first experience. All the weeks of sexual anticipation, of dreams of love, had not prepared me for the swimming sensation, nor the enormity of my response. Lying together, enfolded in close embrace, I breathe raggedly, my body crushed beneath his. He lies upon me, as if pierced by a knife, his weight so heavy, I grow numb.

It is as if we await a return to life? I feel limbless, without appendages, as if hollowed out, but slowly, each nerve end resumes its normal state.

I become aware of my right arm, and painstakingly, I withdraw it, cramped and pricking with pins and needles, as Risto silently rising, pulls on his pants and moves to the pitcher and basin on the washstand in the corner of the studio. He pours water onto a soft washcloth, grabs a towel from the rack, and gently bathes my body, dries it with the towel and proceeds to help me dress.

"You are mine. You always will be," he says, a simple statement.

I am buttoning my blouse.

"Are you hungry?" he asks.

"I don't know. I guess so. Yes. I'm very hungry."

"I have some *gruyère* and *baguette* from this morning – and ah, a little red wine…"

Nothing ever tasted so good. I devour the fresh loaf. We finish it between us, laden with slices of the cheese, and the wine slides down by the glassful.

Through the garden door, the air is sweet with June. The sun glows in its sky. There has never been such a day, at least, never for me.

We talk little. Finally, "Oh, there's the painting I painted over, the one that was Modigliani's."

I see a small canvas on the floor, leaning against the wall, at which he points.

"I brought it out yesterday. I like the cubist, curvilinear way I drew it, don't you? Lot of thick paint."

I do not have a clue what the picture is about…heavy black lines, brilliant purples and reds and greens, in angular shapes.

"I brought it out because I wanted to paint you that way."

"I don't understand."

But Risto is again going on about Modigliani. "Poor bastard. Last time I saw him was the end of 1919 – just before he died. Went to his apartment. He lived in the same building where Gauguin once lived."

"You knew Gauguin?"

"Only slightly…years ago. He was another pathetic case, but a gigantic artist. Modigliani worshipped Gauguin's use of color…so much so, he painted his own rooms in orange and pink and royal blue. He just lay there on his unmade bed in that fantastic Tahitian nightmare, hacking his life away, spitting up blood. It made the death scene spectacularly vivid, the bed cluttered with books and drawings, even sardine cans dripping oil…"

"That's kind of disgusting. Why do you tell me this gruesome story? Is that the end for all artists?"

"One surely hopes not! Just want you to know what you might be getting into with me," he twinkles.

"Sardine cans dripping oil?"

Risto laughs, a deep, booming laugh.

"But Risto, I don't understand. What does Modigliani – and that painting of his you painted over – have to do with your portrait of me?"

"Well, my style – about which you know nothing, my darling. My style in that little painted over canvas – is what I wanted to take a good look at. It brings a lot of money nowadays. But more important, it is used for your disguise."

"My disguise?"

Risto grins at me. "Think a minute. Why would you need to be in disguise?"

"I don't know…"

"Come now, Cammy. Just what do you think your high-minded father would have to say about a picture of his young daughter in the nude…a little Venus on the half shell – eh?"

"He might never have to see it," I say, clamping shut my lips.

"Cammy, please give me credit for being more important than that. I hope everybody will see it. I'm proud of it. I hope it'll bring a large price. And there's someone else who might object?"

"Who?"

"Have I no connections? There is Rose, you know, and Roberto."

He sets down his wine glass. I do the same, paling slightly at the thought of them. I had so easily forgotten.

"I would not want to hurt them," Risto continues in a low voice.

"Nor would I." Somehow, mentioning all these intrusive people that occupy our lives, strips the sheen from my gaiety.

"No, we wouldn't want that." There is silence. "Well," he says, rising to his feet. "Don't you want to see your picture? Remember, it is not your usual nude."

From all this discussion of disguise, I have envisioned a naked lady, with veiled face, or a romantic nude, with the black lines and brilliant color of the painted–over Modigliani. I am hardly prepared for what I see.

As I round the corner of the huge canvas, Risto says, "I'm calling it Still Life."

In the afternoon sunlight, streaming in from the garden, my eyes widen as they come to rest on the enormous picture. It is a series of round globs, outlined heavily in thick, black paint, orbs with nipples, in green and purple, a large yellow pitcher-shape with curving handle, like a female torso. Where the head should be is a white blob on top of a long, white string (the neck?), with three smaller, purple blobs – (two eyes and a nose?). It even has a checkered, diagonal square at the bottom (my silk skirt?).

I do not know whether to laugh and ask, 'Is this some sort of joke?' or dissolve into tears. It is ghastly and incomprehensible to me. Is this the way Risto sees me? Is this his image of love? Green breasts! One yellow, one orange leg! These are mine?

Who would possibly want this garish creation, this me in disguise, much less pay the large price for it Risto expects?

"It's extraordinary," I say, in a horrified voice, lips trembling.

"It's not what you expected, eh?" Risto says with good humor.

"No."

"Cammy, are you about to cry?"

"I'm considering it," I say to be funny, but nature overcomes me, after the shatteringly emotional afternoon, and I give in to a flood of tears.

1927 July Paris

EIGHTEEN

7.

I AM TRYING TO LIVE peacefully at home, on the Avenue Victor Hugo near the Bois de Boulogne. The Lycée d'Athènes has had its traditional ritual for the young ladies successfully completing their final examinations. I do not know how I managed to be one of them, I have been so distracted of late, but I was and I walked through the ceremony unemotionally. Maman was there. Papa was not.

The days, the hot days of July, are long, for Risto is in Cannes with his 'family', *pour les vacances*. A whole month! I imagine the cool Mediterranean, which I have never seen, the bluest and richest of seas, under unfiltered sunshine. Eaten with jealousy, I am constantly on the verge of tears.

I go to the Musée Rodin longingly. I shop, at least with my eyes, in the company of Suzelle. One day in early July, she and I go to the Bois bringing wedges of bread laden with Parma ham, which I am unable to eat. We sit on a bench under the dry and wilted leaves of the alders. Paris is in the throes of a drought. We listlessly watch the swans, and the dying rambler roses, shriveled by the sun. I feel like one of the blossoms.

Even Suzelle has lost her sparkle. Is it through association with such a dour friend as I have become?

"Being 17 isn't as much fun as I'd hoped," she remarks.

"I'll be 18 next week, or have you forgotten? Maybe my age will bring an end to this imprisonment."

"What'll we do to celebrate?" Suzelle says, trying to cheer me. "Something extraordinary, something dangerous." She kicks up her legs, ruffling the dust and coating her brown shoes.

"No, no, nothing. I want no present, no party, no nothing."

Suzelle turns to me. "Where is the laugh you used to laugh so easily? Camille, you've lost it somewhere. If this is what being in love with Risto is doing to you…?"

"Zelle, just stop that!" I say sharply. "It's only because he's away from me…and how can I be expected to be gay with the way I'm living? Avenue Victor Hugo is like an armed camp. No one speaks, much less laughs." I spin a pebble into the little pond before which we sit, where it makes a small plunk.

"You can't go on like this forever!"

"Don't worry. I won't."

Risto has forbidden me to write. Being prevented from expressing my feelings, coupled with living in my house of silence, leaves me frustrated like a muzzled dog unable to bark. I feel between two worlds, two lives. At least I have poetry. Last night I had written a poem about a child with face pressed against a windowpane with longing.

Although I cannot write to Risto, at least I get letters from him. Every morning I screen the *poste*. It usually arrives about 7:00 and is placed in the box beside the wooden door. I am daily to be found there sorting it through in my nightclothes. That alone would give Papa fits… after all, the neighbors! So far I have been lucky, and he has yet to catch me. I seek the large blue envelope with the square writing, the sight of which stops my heart.

In the last letter, received three days ago, Risto had written:

> "My darling little girl: I pine for you. In fact, I don't think
> I can stand it. You may see me sooner than you think!
>
> Lovingly, R"

But that was three days ago. My elation vanished in air by the middle of the same afternoon. Words are just not enough.

"Come on," says Suzelle, breaking into my thoughts. "Let's get an ice. Maybe raspberry."

We make our way to a kiosk, in the square behind us, alive with dusty children playing and calling one another like a bunch of birds. Usually, they do not bother me, but today, I find them loathsome.

"Come. Eat." Zelle is lapping at a pink ice in a paper cone. "It's delicious."

"No, no really. I couldn't."

"What, you're not on a diet?"

"No." In fact, I have lost over a kilo and a half in the few days Risto has been gone, the only fact of his absence that gives me any pleasure.

"I think I'll go back to the barracks," I say. "At least the house will be cooler."

"Already? To your purgatory?"

"Yes," I say with finality.

The house is cooler on my arrival home. Olga lets me in. I am still without a key. Whether or not my parents are aware of Risto's absence from Paris, I do not know.

Olga's brow is wreathed in furrows. In whispers, she says, "Your Maman is upstairs resting...but this came for you, Camille. I managed to intercept it without her knowing, may God forgive me."

She hurries back to her domain after slipping a small envelope in my hand.

It is a *téléphonique* from Cannes to a Paris telephone office, and from thence in an envelope to me.

Suddenly, the day so numbingly hazy, clears like a sky after a rain. The air is cleaner and the birds of the street, instead of wrangling, are singing.

I go to the wing chair in the salon and sit down slowly. I gaze at the envelope, smoothing it on my knees, finally tearing it open with one movement, like a cat swiping at a mouse.

Unfolding the single sheet, I read:

"How would you like me as a birthday present?
Save the day. I'll be there.

R."

The breath is knocked out of me. I am limp in the arms of the great wing chair until, suddenly, avid in the way of a child, I am willing to take the wildest risks.

My first thought is what will I wear? Perhaps the blue dress with the white smocking at the throat…and the cologne he says smells like a flowering meadow and is so natural to me. And I shall bring him a present. Some champagne! I can take it from Papa's cellar. Add thief to my list of attributes, I think ruefully. Papa won't notice. It's so rare he has anything to celebrate. It would still be stealing, but I will consider it Papa's birthday present to me.

I wonder whether my estranged parents are planning anything for my birthday. Turning 18 is important whether we are speaking or not. Since I am in such a bad position with them, I doubt there will be a celebration. In any case, it will not matter. I will be with Risto.

Maman and Papa are planning to go to Dinard on Monday, the day of my birthday, to get out of the heat of the city for 10 days. Dinard is near Saint-Malo on the western coast of France.

They will expect me to accompany them. How will I refuse? What excuse can I give? They cannot drag me, after all.

Suzelle! I must see her right now. We can concoct a ruse. Flinging out the door, I run all the way to her home.

We devise a plan. I will stay at her house with her parents, while my own are in Dinard. We even gain Madame Mauldre's permission for my visit, on the pretext of making plans for the fall, a job, extra courses, perhaps a trip to expand horizons.

"Decisions! Decisions!" I exclaim to Madame Mauldre. She is pleased with this turn of events and commends us for out vitality, 'particularly in this heat', she says, fanning herself. 'Very responsible!' Secretly, I feel she is glad Suzelle will have someone to amuse her for a few days. I have grave reservations my own parents will accept the fiction so gracefully.

On returning to my house, I run down to the cellar and rummage among the racks, finding a champagne I know will please Risto. I return to the foyer to see on the rosewood table, my father's hat. A hat! Even in this weather! He must have returned while I was downstairs. I go quickly to my room and secrete my booty at the far back of the closet, behind shoes, a hatbox and my badminton racquet. I hear my father on the floor below call Olga and tell her to summon me.

She approaches my door, taps gently and with great aplomb, I think, I descend the stairs to the salon. Standing in the center is Papa, in his gray suit and silk foulard, the same clothes he would wear on a winter day. He must be stifling.

He does not greet me.

Instead he says, "I have been to your lover's studio."

I stand in shocked silence before him.

"He wasn't there. In fact, he and his family, the family you so despise, are in the south of France for the month of July. I found out from the concierge. Are you aware of that fact?"

I do not reply.

"I imagine you are. It explains why you've been moping about. It's very lucky for him I didn't find him. But August is another month, and I'll surely see him then."

"And what will you tell him, Papa?"

"I will tell him to leave you alone, of course…you, who are so ripe for dissimulation! He must leave you along."

"And if he will not?"

"Oh, he will. I have a few tricks in my pocket."

"What tricks?" I am alarmed.

"Oh, nothing you really need to know," he replies smugly. "Only little tricks like threatening exposure to his wife…"

"That's blackmail!"

"Blackmail, is it? For a man to protect his daughter? His underage daughter?"

"I'll be 18 in a matter of hours!"

"Risto is doing much worse than blackmail!"

What he suggests would realize Risto's worst fears. Perhaps the truth would be best. It would almost be a relief. Nothing will keep me from Risto. Papa's methods disgust me. Evidently, mine disgust him, for he continues in somber tones.

"Your behavior these past months has been reprehensible. It has your mother and me at wit's end. As you know, we leave Monday for Dinard, a place I remember with fond recollection, because it was there I came to know a little girl named Camille with long blonde tresses and a love for pralines and swimming among the rocks and an infectious spirit, a little girl I have lost." His voice is all sadness.

"Perhaps the little girl has grown up?"

He laughs harshly. "You call your carrying-on grown up?"

Then, moving aimlessly about the room, touching here a lampshade, there, the tasseled fringe of the window curtain, he says, not looking at me, "You will come to Dinard."

"No."

"I expected that would be your response," he says with a deep sigh. "I was hoping you would come and help retrieve that child for us again, hoping we could recapture a family once more. You might even be able to forget your lover and come home where you belong."

"Papa, you ask too much. I don't want to be a little yellow-haired girl any more."

"Dinard might give us time to discuss your future...make plans for the coming year."

"I have plans for the coming year."

"I expected that reply too!"

"Dinard would be wrong for me right now," I continue rapidly. "It would give me too much time to brood about Risto on the lonely beach. I want to stay in Paris."

"You can hardly stay in the house here alone. Olga is taking her week, you know. No! Best you come with us."

"Papa," I say advancing toward him. "I know what you're thinking. But Risto is not here. There's no danger. And truly, I believe a little vacation from one another wouldn't do any of us harm."

"Well, you've certainly got a point there!"

Hope leaps in my breast at this concession.

"I thought maybe you and Maman would let me stay with Zelle. She always puts me in a good mood. You know very well, it needs improving," I say with a smile. "Who knows? She might get me out of this fantasy.

"She's your collaborator."

"With Risto gone, there is nothing to collaborate about."

"Perhaps." He is silent.

"Suzelle and I were talking just today about next year, what we'll be doing. We could begin to firm up some ideas for the future." I say this hopefully.

"Ideas about your artist fellow?"

"No!"

"Monday is your 18th birthday."

"I really don't feel like celebrating this year. For my present, let me stay with Zelle."

"It's an important birthday."

"Then grant this wish."

"You grow more obstinate every day."

"Perhaps I inherit the trait from you."

Papa faces me in the middle of the room. "All right, Camille. Stay with your friend, Suzelle. Don't try to reconcile the family. That's not important enough for you to bother with. Continue with your obsession. I wash my hands of you. God knows, I've tried to get through to you. It's hopeless."

He brushes past me out of the salon, leaving me in the middle of the floor, eyes stinging.

This is the longest exchange of words we have had in months.

For the first time I know I am lost to him…to Maman…even tender Maman. I feel forlorn, as I move to the wing chair where Maman so often sits, and there curl myself into a ball in its depths.

The truth is I love Risto. I belong with him. No matter my parents! No matter my consciousness of guilt! No matter the lies it takes! He is mine. And my birthday belongs to him and to no other, unless it belongs to me!

48 hours later, I am huddled in the stairwell leading to Risto's studio, in my pale blue dress with its lacy front, clutching a bottle of vintage champagne stolen from Papa's cellar and wrapped in brown paper. It is July 12th, my birthday.

People might consider it uncomfortably hot, but to me it is delightful. Risto is coming back to Paris! I wait patiently, having arrived about noon, not knowing exactly when he will get in, for there has been no communication since the *téléphonique*.

I have briefly dropped by the Mauldre's home earlier in the morning, leaving a valise of clothes after Maman and Papa had taken off for Dinard in their motor. I have just as quickly departed on a trumped-up errand – the library, I claim – and Zelle blesses me with a wink.

Finally – it must be almost 4:00 o'clock, Risto appears, a suitcase in one hand. He is burnished brown by the sun of the Midi, and sports a flowing beard. With an enormous smile, he leaps down the stairs and crushes me in an embrace.

I fear for the champagne bottle, which is caught between us, but somehow the thick glass of the bottle manages to hold up against the pressure of the two bodies as we are lost in a long kiss.

We enter and placing the valises and my package on the settee with rapid movements, we embrace again, gradually sinking to our knees, me bending backward almost in half.

This time, I fear for the pressure upon my own body, and unlike the champagne bottle, with its heavy skin of glass, collapse under his weight, succumbing to him on my back on the floor of the studio.

I don't know how it happened. One minute I am upon my feet; the next, on the floor making ferocious love. There was no time in between.

After moments, languidly, we arrange ourselves and rise to sit on the couch. I present him with the beautiful bottle, which draws a protest.

"Ah, Cammy, it is I who should give you gifts, today of all days. But, my dear, you're pale. No sun in Paris? You should be in the south with me...under the golden sky that will turn you to toast and bleach your hair almost white... and one day you'll be there with me, I promise. My God, Cammy, how I've missed you!"

"Now, let's see about this wine. Veuve Cliquot, 1925. Marvelous!" he continues, examining the champagne. "I know there's no ice in the ice chest…but maybe there's some water left in the pitcher that is cool enough to chill it."

He goes to the washstand and there is water left, and he uses the ceramic pitcher on which is painted some brilliant geometrics. With the bottle inside, the pitcher makes a handsome cooler.

"Shall we have supper here?" he asks suddenly. "It's probably more discreet, don't you think?"

"I suppose," I reply, "although Maman and Papa are out of Paris. They believe you're not here. It's the only reason they dared leave me behind. Papa paid you a visit last week, by the way."

"That's nice." Risto says dryly and makes a grimace as if in pain.

"When he found you gone, he let me stay in the city at my friend, Suzelle's."

Risto turns to me with delight. "You'll stay here with me! Cammy, we'll have a whole night of love. I feel like it's my birthday too."

"What about the Mauldres? They'll certainly tell my parents eventually. Besides, they'll worry."

"You care more for the Mauldres than you do for me? You're breaking my heart. Surely we can think of something. It's not yet 5:00. Perhaps we could send them a *téléphonique*. How about 'I want to be with my lover', he twinkles at me.

"Oh, Risto. Perhaps if I went there and saw Suzelle…but no. She'd be totally against it because it would get her in trouble too."

"Well, my love, you think. I will go to the charcuterie and pick up some things for supper…and for breakfast, mind you…so think hard."

With that he is gone.

I wander about the large room. It is the dusky time of day –*le crépuscule*, a time of light that precedes nightfall. Purple shadows are lengthening. There is a poignant smell from the garden outside, the smell of dampness before rain, of flowers when the days of flowers are past, a premonition of an autumn still far away.

I am in a limbo state, a region on the border of heaven. I have come up against what one meets only once in a lifetime. I touch the pictures on the floor and on the walls. Their tactile feel, the impact of their brilliant color, brings me to a reality I understand. I know I must follow my feelings. I have no choice.

Risto returns with a flurry, heaped with parcels and waving a large *baguette.*

"Anyone you know?" He throws the bread to me in a gentle arc. Laughing, we settle down to slices of county *paté* with rough, strong flavors and our tepid champagne.

The Mauldres are not mentioned again this night. I do not think of them at all.

Risto tries a variety of love experiments with me, in the shadowy room, doors open to the garden, cool night air laving us. Lit by one candle, our single silhouette moves, changes and rechanges, reflected in the cracked mirror.

The dawn brings me to the back garden doors in a state of exhaustion, conscious of the fact I now possess the mystery of physical love…and conscious of little else.

THE GIFT

8.

I SIT BESIDE RISTO, STUDYING that face, careful not to disturb him. I put my arms on each side of his body and press my forehead against his, seeking to enter his dreams. I seem to see his visions.

With my movement, he speaks. Just one word.

"Cammy."

"Forgive me. I was so busy looking at you, I must have jostled you."

"It doesn't matter. There you are," he says, rearing up on his elbows. "So beautiful…so much mine!"

The aftermath of our loving is as intense as the passion, and we await the tide to recede. Knowledge is mine and innocence is gone. Nothing in me exists any longer that dates back before Risto.

After the ritual of washing each other, I start to don my chemise, but Risto stays my hand.

"Oh, please, wait I want to draw you and me together."

He removes the cracked mirror from the wall, balances it on a straight chair opposite the couch, and we both lie among the cushions nude together, his arm about me. We are reflected in the mirror, in which he gazes with a practiced eye. Then leaping up with a "Don't move!" he grabs drawing paper and a piece of charcoal. Standing up, rapidly sketching away by the open door to the garden, he works quickly. It goes on for many minutes. By this time I am almost asleep, head thrown back, one arm arced above it, clutching a pillow.

In fact, I do sleep and awake to find him sitting beside me proudly, laughing elfishly, and when finally I am roused, he presents me with not one picture, but two.

"This I shall call Artist and Model at Rest," he says. It is a graphic nude pair, not in the least like Still Life, but realistic and detailed, showing the two of us, he with his beard, looking like a satyr, and me with breasts enlarged and raised. It is in black and white, with the double doors to the garden at the back of the picture.

"You know, I like it," he says firmly. "Might do a series of etchings on this one day. Would you help me?"

I smile with joy at the prospect.

The second drawing is a picture of me asleep, head thrown back. It is just the outline, done like a molten oval, the charcoal heavy and black. My body is one smooth curve like the edge of a rhododendron leaf. It is very round.

"And this," he says, presenting it to me, Nude on a Flowered Couch."

"Am I really so fat?" I say with alarm. "Am I so…so…round?"

"It's the way I see you, luscious, all accepting, ready to embrace everything I wish for you. It looks the way you feel when I make love to you."

"At least, I can recognize myself more easily than in Still Life." I feel a small victory. Risto has risked my disguise.

"They are beautiful," I say truthfully. "Oh, I wish I could have them." But knowing the need for secrecy, I recognize the impossibility of such a proposal. Just where would I put them?

I rise and continue dressing, interrupted some hours ago. I boil water for the *café filtre* on the small gas grill, suddenly ravenous.

"Cammy, I must get some fresh milk, and perhaps I can find a croissant or two, eh? I'll only be a minute."

"Hurry, please. I'm starved."

He is off in one stride.

Taking a mug of the steaming, black liquid, I go to the glass doors and sit on the stoop into the garden. It is a morning, boding rain.

18! And a woman for sure! I smile at the garden, watching the small sparrows grubbing for food in its dusty tangle. 18! Seeing the dust rise from beneath a bush where a bird is pecking, I think of Suzelle's brown shoe in the park, covered with pale dirt, where she had scuffed it in the air, and my heart drops to the pit of my stomach.

I have forgotten the Mauldres – completely – and my parents. More urgent, the Mauldres! They must be in a panic at my disappearance, at my never returning from the 'library'. What if they should call the police? I can see the headlines. MISSING 18 – YEAR-OLD – On the Day of Her Birthday!

I wish Risto were here. He would know what to do. It is more than an hour since his departure. I begin to pace.

I am just plain scared. Not such a woman after all. I am nothing but a frightened little girl. When I think this, I start to cry. I think of Maman, dear Maman, trusting me, loving me, even blessing me. Now, I am sobbing.

Risto, finally returned to the studio, finds the radiant girl he left huddled on the couch, weeping and wringing her hands.

"Cammy! What's happened?" he exclaims, dropping his packages, Le Journal, and several letters on the divan, in a heap beside me.

"Why are you crying?"

"I've been thinking of Maman, and Papa, and above all, the Mauldres! They might have even gone to the police!"

Risto blanches.

"They are responsible people, and I was put in their charge. We've got to do something," this last in a wail.

"Calm down, now Cammy. Let me think a minute." Risto is walking aimlessly about.

"Let's see. What if you go there right now and apologize and explain…It's a problem…after your errand yesterday…the excuse was the library, wasn't it?...you returned home to pick up a book and your parents hadn't yet left for Dinard…not until this morning. Being your birthday, you celebrated together and simply forgot. As your parents are already out of the city, it's unlikely the Mauldres would check."

"If they'll only believe me…"

"Throw yourself on their mercy. Be an actress, something you already are. And be very apologetic for causing their worry. Now, hurry. The sooner, the better. Let's get it over with. And when you're done, come back to me. I have a present for you." And Risto pushes me out the entry door, rather brusquely, before I have a chance to think.

He is certainly in a hurry, I say to myself, and I am rather disgruntled by the thought that, on top of the pile of letters on the divan is one with florid script and the postmark, Cannes. Rose!

It is not so easy. The Mauldres are in consternation over my defection and truly close to taking the matter to the police.

"We thought you kidnapped, even!" Madame Mauldre, plump in her black bombazine – in July? – exclaims with fear in her eyes.

Suzelle looks haggard, having spent a night of sleepless imaginings,

"You know how much worse it is at night, Cammy. I had you drowned in the Seine, for heaven's sake." And she hugs me.

My explanation seems to stand, perhaps because of their relief, although Madame Mauldre says in quizzical wonderment, her eyes enormous in the little round face. She has Zelle's ferret teeth. "It's so unlike your mother, not to let us know."

To which I quickly reply, "But you see it was my birthday. They decided to stay, and we got so carried away, you've no idea. You know, I'm 18 and that's a momentous day for anyone. They couldn't bear to not share it with me. Forgive me…forgive all of us," I continue in supplicating tones, all the while marveling at how easy it is to lie.

Later, with Zelle, I tell the truth – up to a point – that I have been alone with Risto in his studio, and that I absolutely must return. His present is waiting.

Suzelle wails, "Mama won't let you out of her sight. How could you leave me in such a position, Camille? Last night was a nightmare. They almost had me believing you dead, even though I was pretty sure where you were – and what you were doing." Her voice drops.

"Why, Zelle, you're shocked? It's much more innocent than you think," I continue to lie. "And I must go back, just for a couple of hours. I promise no repeat of last night. We can tell your mother I forgot something at the house."

"Where do you get the 'we'?" Zelle says sullenly. "You tell her. You've got to promise to be back as soon as you can. I don't think I can survive another night like the last one.

"I promise."

Somehow I manage to return to Risto's studio. It is now early afternoon, and I am hungrier than I ever remember being. All I have had is some strong, black coffee at dawn.

Risto is not there. The studio is locked. I am suddenly sorry for myself, when I spy him across the street, in front of a small building next to the charcuterie. He is talking to a fat woman, shakes hands with her, and the woman gives him something. Then Risto comes rapidly toward me, across the street to the studio.

"How'd it go?" he says, hugging me to him and unlocking the studio door.

"All right, I guess. They seemed to accept it, although Madame Mauldre can't believe my mother would let them stew in a sea of worry all night. She's right. Maman wouldn't! But I must be back soon. No overnight visit tonight."

"I understand," he says, with a grin, "and since you're in a hurry, we'll get to your surprise!"

He takes my hand and draws me out of the studio. We cross the street and walk past the pastry shop where *baguettes* lie in woven baskets in the window and cakes catch my hungry eye. We pass the boot black. No sustenance there. We go past Héberd's Bookshop with its three steps leading below street level to the entrance, like Risto's studio and almost directly opposite it. Next to Héberd's is the charcuterie with dishes of cold salads and terrines on display, so enticing I am salivating.

Adjoining that delectable shop is Number 44, rue La Boëtie. We enter its double door, after first ringing. The concierge in her room near the entrance, releases the bolt. We go through a dark hall and up broad, wooden stairs to the top of the building's three floors. On the landing, there is only one door, a black one, which Risto unlocks with a key.

We enter a vestibule, almost circular in shape, pass a tiny kitchen to the left and enter, on the right, a long room with a fireplace at the far end. There are three windows looking out on the inner courtyard and the street beyond; a bright rug on the floor in shades of blue. There is a rather lumpy couch against the wall opposite the windows between which are a table and two chairs.

The table is set with several dishes, trembling eggs in jelly; bread; a round, red, Dutch cheese; wine. Before we partake of these, we go through a door to the left of the fireplace and enter a bedroom. There is a huge, brass, four-poster bed almost filling the room, a window at the back looking out on a scruffy garden, next to which is the door to a lavatory and dressing room with a tall window.

"Well," says Risto, "What do you think?"

"What do you mean, 'what do I think'?"

Turning around in the center of the bedroom, I see between the two brass posts at the head of the bed hanging on the wall, Artist and Model at Rest. Nude on a Flowered Couch is on the far wall. The pictures are startling in their eroticism, lending this rosy bedroom an ambiance of sensual abandon.

"The pictures," I breathe. "They're perfect here. But why ARE they here? Why are WE here? Are you moving?"

Risto laughs. "You really don't understand? Cammy, this is yours. It's my gift to you on your 18th birthday. It's your liberation, a present to keep you near me. It's your new home."

I sink down on the pink coverlet.

"You're joking."

"Hardly." Risto sits beside me and takes my hand. "This will be our haven. You can live here as much as you want… all the time, I hope. It may take a while to make the transfer from Avenue Victor Hugo. Anyway, it's yours…ours…an island…a place we can be together."

With these remarks, he drops the shining key into my open palm. Number 44, rue La Boëtie. This is to be an island of love? Number 23, rue La Boëtie is right across the street, so close, in fact, I can see into the third floor windows.

Such a tandem position! So uncomfortably near to his home! So near to Rose! So near to Roberto! One day would I see them on the street, she in her leotards and Roberto with a toy? Would I see them, through the window, at table in their third floor flat, dining together, all three? Would I see Risto kiss her goodbye on her way to the theater?

"I'm hungry."

It is all I can say on this bright July afternoon, the afternoon of my 18th birthday, but as time passes, I begin to accept the inevitability of my addiction. There are moments in the black of night when I tremble at what I do. So thoughtfully reared by parents who care intensely, I am drifting into seas with hidden currents. Risto, a magnetic moon, pulls me to him from the safety of my home.

Maman and Papa represent the stableness of the land itself, placid, programmed and unexciting.

I don't doubt their love, Maman's all encompassing, Papa's laced with rigid demand. As I begin my tentative foray into what I consider to be adult life, they seem to recede from me, grow dimmer. They barely speak, Maman, because of her horrified disapproval, and Papa! I do not think he wants me to grow to womanhood at all.

But Risto does. Oh yes! He knows women. He loves women. He loves them so much, it brings to me a chill terror that I might merely be his woman of the moment!

There must be ways to make a man love you forever, even a man such as Risto. I will never lose him. This is the vow I make at night, sometimes in the narrow bed at Avenue Victor Hugo, more and more frequently in the deep four-poster of 44, rue La Boétie.

And what of the world? What will it do to me when it discovers, as it surely must, we are lovers. The world does not take kindly to a young, unmarried girl living openly with a man with a family, a man so much older. I wonder exactly how old he is. The world always demands an eventual rejection.

But this will not happen to me. Risto will not discard me. I trust him – with my person, my love, my existence. I will cleave to him always. I will stimulate and influence. He already speaks often of that special inspiration I bring him, at once, both sensual and ethereal.

Yet, in the blackness of my night terrors I wonder. I remember Rodin's peasant woman. I remember the beautiful Camille Claudel. Once each was inspiration too.

1927 Late September Paris

44, RUE LA BOËTIE

9.

It is hard to define
The line
Where dreams begin.

IF THERE IS ANY true line of definition for a dream, it is marked right here at 44, rue La Boëtie. When Risto enters, I fly to him. I give him large doses of love. He comes to me at least once a day. Sometimes it is only for morning coffee.

On certain afternoons, I go across to his studio to make love and then be painted. Most often, he comes here around 8:00 in the evening, and we twine together sharing love and laughter and food and his latest project until exhausted, he rises from my bed, grumbling and tousled, and makes his way across the street. It is only after his departure that I, sleepy with love, sense through my luxuriant lassitude, the shadows that will surely come.

One such shadowed moment occurs in the form of a ringing bell and the rounded figure behind the door. Maman! I pale before her as she enters the living room without a word of greeting, eyes straight ahead and seats herself. A long moment ensues while she removes the gloves, retrieves the handkerchief from the handbag, and relaxes the body sufficiently to sink back in the chair. I run to close the bedroom door.

Silence!

"The happiest day of my life was the day I first held you...the brightest and best...of all my years."

Maman's round blue eyes are half shut in memory, impossible to see into, fringed with their dark lashes. Her neatly coiffed head is leaning against the plum cushion of the one decent chair in the salon with its gaudy-shabby décor.

I have kept her from entering the bedroom with door firmly closed. The bed alone would upset her. But the pictures of me nude would be so offensive as to make her depart in bitter distress. Such concrete evidence! Such an affront to dignity, to herself, and to her daughter and, of course, most of all to her beloved Gerard, my father, of whom, in fact, she is mortally afraid.

"Camille, what did we do wrong? I think you were the dearest, sweetest little girl I ever saw. Always so willing, so eager, with such a capacity for fun."

I say nothing.

"You were solemn too. You were the silent child I used to watch in church gazing up at the altar, awaiting some miracle, perhaps a smile from the Virgin's lips. You were so believing in miracles."

"I still am."

"This passion of yours?"

"It's pure."

"Pure! How can you use that word – in here – in this," Maman says waving her hand at the over-decorated room. "I cannot believe my eyes. It isn't just – this –" again the hand, "but what it represents. Dear Camille. What can I do? Only tell me. I'll do anything."

I am voiceless.

"Have you any idea of the punishments society visits upon the demi-monde woman? That is exactly what you are...in the half-light, not respectable, living somewhere beneath society, open to gossip. Have you any idea of the punishments inflicted on the family of that woman as well?"

Two fat tears slowly descend each cheek, the eyes now shut tight.

"Do you know your father barely speaks?"

"How is Papa?" I feel a terrible twinge.

"He's so tense, so silent, almost unrecognizable. We never entertain. We see practically nobody. It is stifling and lonely. I am so sad."

Abruptly, her eyes fly open.

"Camille, I don't say this to make you feel more guilty than you already must…but I beg you to come home. It won't wipe out the disgrace, but it would contain it, keep it from growing more public. I beg you to come home from the bottom of my heart. Where is the girl I knew? How did she become this new Camille?"

"I can't go home. And it is not a 'new' Camille you see. It is the same old one," I say.

"It's not." Maman sits up, working her handkerchief. "It's someone I don't even know, so stubborn, so careless of others. Just why can't you reverse the way you're living?"

"It's too late."

"What do you mean?" Maman says, round eyes widening in horror, reflecting her unthinkable question.

"I'm as much committed as if I were married. I can't direct the course of love. It directs me. I have no will in the matter."

"I don't believe that," she says, looking relieved I'm not pregnant. "One always has one's will – and in your case, maybe too much. What about Madame Risto? Isn't she, too, committed?"

"I care nothing for her. And she doesn't know of my existence."

"Well, that's only a matter of time, surely." Maman rises to her feet and goes to my vigil-window, where I spend many an hour peering at the third floor window of 23, rue La Boëtie diagonally across the street.

"They live across there, don't they?" she says softly.

"Yes."

"So close?"

"Yes."

"How can you stand it?" she says, turning to me.

"Because I must."

"Are you so docile, then? Where's your pride? Have you...no second thoughts...no searching of soul?"

"I dream on many nights of my...my position...and of yours and of Papa's and of her's and of the little boy's. Sometimes, it's a terrible dream...a doll with her stuffing sticking out, or a single rose with its blossom lopped off and lying in the dust."

I pause and gloomily play with the gold tassels on one of the worn-out cushions on the couch.

"Maman," I continue. "I have no choice. This man gives me life... even more than Papa did in siring me."

"Don't say that!"

"Oh, Maman." I rise to go to her. "I know I'm not noble. I know I'm not strong. But with all my present position, I know I'm decent. I know my love is pure. You and Papa did nothing wrong in my upbringing to make this happen. It just did. I cannot even say I choose to live this way I can only say 'I live this way.'"

Maman stares at me searchingly for a long time. There is sorrowful acceptance in her gaze. That's something. Then, gathering her gloves, she impulsively hugs me.

"Will you come to see your father?"

"To what purpose, Maman? The last violent scene between us had nearly given him a seizure and almost made me faint. "What more can be said?"

"Perhaps you're right." She hugs me again. "Remember, Camille, I am always your mother. You could commit murder and I would be there for you. Perhaps that's where I went wrong."

And she is gone.

I am alone again, remembering. This is the only time I have seen my mother since that last ghastly confrontation more than six weeks ago in early August.

I had been at the house on Victor Hugo, that sweltering early August afternoon in my room packing a valise with the lightest clothing I could find, my notepad and pencils, some booklets of my poems in spirally script, a bottle of cologne, and a small photograph of Maman and Papa in a gilt frame. It had been taken at Dinard, two years ago, by a beach photographer. They are smiling, standing close against the rocks, Maman in a white cotton dress, Papa in a boater.

Stuffing these possessions into the case, I descended the stairs as quietly as possible, passed the salon on cat's feet, glancing into the room to see Papa – at this mid-afternoon hour? – uncharacteristically slumped in the large wing chair, head down and brooding. As I reached the outer door in the foyer, his voice issued forth, clarion-clear.

"Camille."

I set the valise down, heart fluttering in my chest, and returned to the entrance of the living room, its shades pulled to keep in the coolness, and approached him to stand before him.

"Just what deceit are we up to now?"

"I beg your pardon?"

"Don't lie, Camille."

"How begging your pardon is lying, I don't know."

"Don't be insolent. Just where were you going with your valise?"

I just stood there.

"Answer me...or may I guess." He raised malevolent eyes to my face. "Could it be to your hide-away, courtesy of Monsieur Risto? I believe it's number 44, on the same street he lives with his wife and child. Most convenient."

How had my father found out?

"Yes, Camille. I know it all. I'm ashamed to say, it has been necessary with your behavior which is...grotesque, to have you under surveillance, for the past weeks..."

"You wouldn't!"

"Oh, but I would! I already have. As an insurance broker, I have access to all manner of detecting facilities. You left me no option. We're not dealing with just you – but with your Mother and myself and somebody else's wife and child – all of whom you seem to ignore. I felt impinged upon to try and protect all these various people from your destructiveness."

I said nothing as he went on.

"Aside from all these others, whose reputations and peace of mind are being ruined by your selfishness, consider that vey self – you – for a moment. You know the old phrase, 'What have I got to lose?' In your case, what in God's name, have you got to win?"

"It isn't a case of lose or win."

"What is it a case of, then? Obsessive sex? Desire to be 'grown-up?' a much misguided desire, I might say. The whole thing is shocking."

"It's a case of love," I said almost inaudibly, at which my father had burst into chilling laughter, far more soulshrinking than further reprimand would have been.

"Ah, love," he said, almost choking, turning quite red in the face. "That's your name for an illicit, whorish pattern you have been developing, lo these many months, sneaking about, lying, leading a second life, thinking you have fooled us, your parents, who have been nothing but good to you. I won't speak of gratitude. Let's forget that. Where is the person you were, I want to know, with some ideals and ideas of her own? Where did she disappear to, and how was she so easily replaced by an overheated ninny?"

Risto had called me a ninny once under different circumstances.

"You are nothing but an object for that man to paw. My own daughter!" Papa said. "And do you see what he's got at his temples? White hairs, Camille, white hairs...like mine!"

If Risto had white hairs, I had never noticed them.

"You are nothing but an object for him to use," Papa continued to rant, "to vent his sex upon, a toy, a creature who waits for him like some slave girl in a bad Turkish harem. And you permit this? Hardly. You lap it up!"

"You make it sound so dirty. You don't understand, Papa. He makes me feel important and loved. He even needs me in his work – in his artistic creation."

I had not let him interrupt.

"When I am with Risto, life takes on a glow – and the time together – I don't know where it goes. It curls through my fingers like the mist - suddenly gone."

"Stop it. Stop it right now."

Papa was on his feet and truly bright red.

"I can't listen to this, Camille. All these excuses for behaving like a common street tart! You say you are involved in his 'artistic' creation? What garbage! Do you mean he has convinced you to pose without clothes on the grounds it's for his art?"

Maman had suddenly appeared in the doorway, her face alarmed.

"I heard such loud voices. What is going on?"

"It's this idiot daughter of yours. She has her valise. Guess where she is going? Do you know she poses naked for him now?" Papa yelled at her.

"Oh, Gerard, please...don't shout. It gets us nowhere, and you look so red. Try to be calm...please."

"How can I when your daughter is a whore!" he screamed. "How can I be calm? Well, let her go. In fact, I insist she go. I don't want to see her or touch her or talk to her again." With that last phrase at high pitch, and he just seemed to topple to the floor. There was a soft thud.

Maman had let out a shriek and rushing to him, undid the collar and tie at his throat, tears starting from her eyes. I stood transfixed.

"Camille," Maman called. "For God's sake, help me." Papa was panting hard. His face was purple and the tongue seemed to protrude from between pale lips. His body quivered as if from an electric shock.

I ran to him. Maman and I were both on our knees beside his body. I saw his eyelashes tremble.

"Water," he panted, which had made me leap to my feet, go to the kitchen to return with a tumbler, spilling all the way.

Maman had managed to get him onto the wing chair, and together we saw to it some water slid down his throat.

Gradually, his breathing subsided. Then, glaring hard at my mother, not acknowledging my existence, he said in the lowest voice I had ever heard him use, and very slowly,

"Get her out of here!"

Maman merely nodded at me.

I had staggered to the door, like a spastic child so weak I thought I would at any moment collapse in a bundle on the floor. Grabbing my valise, I opened the heavy front door and was met by a blast of heat that threatened to knock me off my feet. Somehow, I found myself at 44, rue La Boëtie once again.

That was more than six weeks ago, and until this day, I have seen neither of my parents. Maman, today, came to some sort of terms with my situation, loving Maman, who dimly understands the call of the heart.

But Papa? He is another question. Will I ever see him again? He doesn't want any part of his only child. He wants her gone forever from his sight, banned from his presence to wallow in her own filth. I wonder, in a kind of agony, why he never did expose me to Rose, or confront Risto. Was he afraid? Did he lack conviction or was it just easier for him to throw me out?

Images pass like shadows, vivid images of summer days on the rocks of Dinard, where a yellow-haired girl collected shells with her stiff, young father in his bathing suit with a striped tank top; or at nearby Le Mont-Saint-Michel, dug in the sand when the tide was out for clams and oysters and sea urchins, or walked in the evening, from the vacation villa, through the main thoroughfares to buy fresh fruit and pralines, the man leading the child by the hand.

1928 Winter Paris

MADEMOISELLE RUY

10.

I AM KNOWN TO THE concierge of 44 rue La Boëtie as Mademoiselle Ruy, as well as to the tradespeople behind the counters at the greengrocers, the bakery, the charcuterie. I am known to the coalman, the iceman, and the postman by this soubriquet. Of course, Ruy is Risto's given name, his first name, and his gift to me. His artist's name, Risto, is borne by the lady across the street.

I saw her – one day last week – a cool, slim lady with regal walk, and sleek, dark hair pulled into a chignon. I noticed that the tendons in her calves under the black stockings were knotty, not smooth and creamy like my own. The encounter took place in the charcuterie, which I had just entered, where she was purchasing *paté de campagne* and Dijon mustard.

"It is always a pleasure," beamed the red-faced proprietor. "Always a pleasure, Madame Risto."

I left the shop with a start, and rushed up the stairs to my apartment, taking up my vigil at the window. There she was, wending her way from shop to shop, like a bee culling pollen. Her features looked taut, and from that angle the nose seemed overly long, maybe a legacy from her Russian heritage. I could not deny an elegance about her person, so sure of herself and of her position in the world.

When Risto showed up later that same evening, I greeted him with 'I know what you had for dinner tonight, *paté de campagne* and Dijon mustard', in rather bitter tones. He was decidedly not pleased.

Today, I sit for a long time in a gray-all-over mood, the salon with its bright colors, dimming around me as the afternoon wanes.

It is hard to define
The line
Where dreams begin.
Goodness and sin,
Sea and sky,
Have more distinction, it seems,
Than dreams.

I write these words, curled up in a corner of the divan. Sin. Am I sinful? I am lonely, that is a certainty. Is loneliness sin in itself? Chastity brings loneliness too, and I am hardly chaste, although my lustfulness applies to only one human being.

I write a lot in the notebook, in my velvet chrysalis. I write standing up at the kitchen table, or with the book open on the mantelpiece. I even write in the bathtub. I am lucky to have such a modern convenience. It is square and deep, and my knees come up to my chin. I balance the notebook on my dry knee-tops. Sometimes the paper gets wet.

Dreams? I am living one, a truly isolated dream, with only one star to brighten it. I am alienated from my family – especially Papa. And Maman has not been to visit me, except for that one time in September when she left us both with broken hearts.

Even Suzelle has ostracized me, although she came for lunch one November day. How stilted she had been, in her hat with blue flowers, the ferret teeth concealed behind disapproving, pursed lips. She had chattered stiffly, showing signs of animation only when discussing a young man named Roger, with whom she was conducting a proper affair; Suzelle, so gifted at sowing the seeds of gaiety, whose words could be as stimulating as cognac, was becoming a bore.

I am sure it was only curiosity that prompted Zelle to see me. She made it very clear, her parents were not to know of her visit. And certainly not Roger!

I am hungry. It was all I could say that day in July, the day of my 18th birthday. Hungry is a strange word. It applies to food of course. It applies to love too. It applies to security. Being between two worlds, I constantly hunger.

Risto cannot fill it this moment. He is not here. When I am with him, time seems gone before it starts. When he leaves me, I am alone again, each parting a small death.

I toss my notebook to the far end of the couch. The sound of a melody, played on a guitar, drifts through the room, 'Jurame' – Swear to Me – a song that rose from Spain last year and became the rage. The wistful music drifts through this gaudy room and twines about the gold candelabra, sticks to the gilt on the picture frames, crawls into the iron grate and burns with the dim fire.

I go to the window. In the winter light, there is the outline of the buildings with their familiar chimney pots. My eyes gaze through the window pane to the third floor of my opposite number across the street, to the apartment with its voile curtains, drawn, with a glow shining through. Shadows move behind them, small movements of darker light that seem to make the fabric ripple.

I construct a scene within my mind, a domestic landscape with fire and books, and paintings of course, a child by the firelight, and raindrops from above.

"Don't ever say, 'that could be you over there'," I say out loud.

Returning to the couch and my notebook, I sit and await his footsteps on the stair. Will he come this night as he has so often? But just as often, he has not. All I hear is the echoing silence, filled with small ticks and creaks, and the subdued melody from below.

I rise and go into the rosy bedroom which now smells of clay. Risto has taken over my dressing room, which has a window facing north. It gives strong, lofty light. He is creating a sculptured head in clay, a head modeled after my own.

Risto has titled the sculpture. Head of a Girl, and although I often go across the street to his studio, he has chosen to make me sit on a small stool in the dressing room by my bedroom where the sunbeams strike my left profile, for this particular project. The clay smell has become a permanent fixture in my sleeping quarters.

"The light. It's so clear," he says. "Perfect!"

After working, he is frequently so exhilerated, he pulls me off the stool and draws me from the dressing room to the bed. Fumbling with clothing, I am lost once again to the overwhelming vitality for which I hunger.

The face of Head of a Girl emphasizes two features; a nose (mine?), curved and strong; the mouth, gently open. They are not recognizable as my own features. They protrude from three rounded forms, the two cheeks and the chignon at the back of the head. To me, they look like male and female sexual organs, particularly if I look upside down, the rounded orbs forming buttocks and thighs. It is not one of my favorite visions of myself, but Risto plans to do a whole series of me sitting on that rough wooden stool.

In the lavatory, I prepare to take a bath in the square tub, the water loaded with scent to overcome the clayey smell permeating my private quarters. I remove my wool dress and throw it on top of the black form in the center of the quilt on my bed, wagging his scruffy tail, a rag/tag gypsy of a dog I have named Frère. This is his favorite spot, one where he nestles in, quiet and warm. It is where he had secreted himself on Maman's visit, last September. A dog as my roommate would have seemed to her the ultimate insult.

Frère...little brother. It is hard to tell of which breed he is, with his rough black coat, legs too long, feet too big, and whiskers like the antennae of some wild insect, all askew. The eyes, brown and dancing, laugh with pleasure.

Frère is a gift from Risto... "to be your companion," he said, that night in August after the dreadful scene at my parents, when Papa collapsed.

"Frère is your new family," he had said, and as I looked at the sorry little dog, I thought, 'what rubbish'! How could this wiggly creature fill my heart, so empty of my parents, aching as if pummeled physically by their fists? Maman's nod for me to leave had been as rejective as all Papa's words.

That night in August, Risto had found me sitting in a darkened room. I had been so engrossed in bitter thoughts, I did not even hear his footsteps on the stair. Entering with his key, he had said, "Cammy, I can't see a thing. Where are you?"

"Here," and suddenly, I had found myself in his arms, in the dark, sobbing out my misery upon his chest. It ended in a tearful love bout that dried my tears. Then Risto had lit the lamps, made me strong coffee, patted me on the hair, and said, "You wait here. Don't move. I'm going to get you a special present." He had returned in what seemed a matter of minutes, with the shaggy black dog under his arm.

"It's a male," Risto said with a laugh. "One bitch in the family is enough, eh?" he said pulling me to him. "And remember, I am your family too…I and this small black canine."

Frère. If he is to be substitute for a family I no longer possess, he might as well be the brother I have always longed for. Risto is the rest.

Frère enters my life, consumes my days and fills the daily tasks with love. He gives me a semblance of routine. We eat breakfast together, go shopping together, take long walks together. He sleeps in my bed, unless it is otherwise occupied. Frère and I love each other. Risto was right. The little dog helps fill the void of my isolation. Where Risto is the day and the night, where he is life, Frère becomes a part of me, the hour that passes by and I have a family again.

1928 Winter Paris

HÉBERD'S

11.

Frère is not Risto's only gift. In effect, I am kept. Risto has installed me here and pays the rent. He also brings food and flowers. He gives me pin money, and it really has been barely enough for pins, so I decide to go to work. Aside from the money, which is becoming a necessity, it will keep me from brooding.

There are two major problems. One: If I have any training or preparation at all from the Lycée, it is in terms of being a 'finished' young woman; in other words, it is in the art of marrying. We were supplied with the rudiments of mathematics, a smattering of literature, language, and music, but we are hardly fitted to earn a living.

The second problem is Frère...what to do with him during days of occupation outside of the flat. He cannot be left to himself for hours.

Just exactly at what would I be working? Let's start with what I like? Badminton – the park – poetry, of course...books. I love books. They have been the largest part of my young intellectual life to date. Perhaps a bookstore. It would be a challenge.

But where? Héberd's? Right down the street next to the charcuterie. I pass it every day.

One cold day in January, just one year from my meeting with Risto in front of the Galeries Lafayette, there is a brutal wind and ice slick on the street. But the sun is strong enough to warm a person if one stands directly in its light. I pause at the door of number 44, on the street warming myself in that pale sun against a numbness that is not only caused by the wind, but by fear. I'm on my way to Héberd's to present myself for a job.

I have dressed carefully. The navy wool skirt and coat of the Lycée are still presentable and not too juvenile. Besides, I have no money to buy other. I have invested, however, in a white blouse with a silk tie in bright green and a matching green cap.

I enter the small bookstore, down the stairs through a grilled door, which tolls a bell on entering. It is dark, a bit musty, but not at all unpleasant.

There are rows and rows of books, going all the way to the high ceiling, with its cream color, tin façade printed with the *fleur de lis*. Two moveable ladders, attached to railings, run the length of the room so one can reach the topmost volumes.

There seems to be a special section for the most expensive books, the ones in leather with gold tooling. I touch them with reverence. Most of the shelves are covered with books in heavy, beige paper covers, the titles in dark letters.

As I enter this dim world, an old gentleman, alerted by the bell, emerges from a back room with a glass window in its door. He is plump, with spectacles on his nose, and a dark vest. I notice he is wearing carpet slippers.

"May I be of help?"

"I don't know," I answer politely.

"What is it you wish?"

"Well, sir, my name is Mademoiselle Camille Ruy, and I live just down the street. At number 44. And, well, sir, I was wondering if there might be a position in your shop. You see, I love books," I blurt, warming to my sales pitch, which I had practiced in front of the mirror over my bathtub in the flat. "And I also need a bit of extra money... anything you would have me do is just fine."

"My goodness! I hardly expected this," he replies, not unkindly. "I am Héberd, by the way...been here for almost 30 years, right here on this spot. But tell me, what can you do?" He regards me with a wise man's gaze.

"Well, sir, I attended the Lycée – the one over near Les Invalides, and I write poetry. My best subject was literature, particularly 18th century," I say, having read recently in Le Journal, that that period is highly popular at the moment.

"That's all very well, but I am not sure how I can use you. This is not an extremely busy shop…just some regular old clients and a few drop-ins…not really enough for a regular salesperson."

"Perhaps I could help with your cataloguing," I jump in. "I'm good at that."

"Well, that's a thought…but there's really not enough work for someone full time."

"What about part-time? Would you at least think about it? Please. You see, I'm alone. I have no family left."

I see his eyes widen in sympathy. I have not meant to use this kind of ploy and except for Frère – and of course, Risto – it's true. I really have no family left. Feeling guilty, I quickly say: "Would you at least consider it? Perhaps I could come back tomorrow for your decision."

Monsieur Héberd sighs, removes his glasses, which he shines with a pocket handkerchief, and says, "Well, all right. Perhaps I could use an extra pair of hands. My office needs a good cleaning out, and the books do get dusty. Also the bookkeeping…yes, come tomorrow, about the same time. I'll give you my decision then, eh?"

I run home elated, leash Frère, and we bound out into the icy wind.

A bargain has been struck. Not for sure – maybe, but there's hope. I will tell Risto this evening. He is planning to come for a late supper. He will be proud of me.

And supper? What should I prepare? I am not a skilled cook, but I certainly can make a small chicken *rôti*. And a salad with some fresh mushrooms sliced in. He loves them. And of course, bread and wine and cheese – a beautiful white *Gourmandise*. I have just enough money to pay for this. There is bread from this morning and, besides, by tomorrow, I am convinced I will be making money! Why not spend all that I have now.

I am not prepared for the disastrous evening that follows, crushing my elation to pulp. Risto is violently upset at the idea of my going to work.

"Why?" I ask him anxiously over the bones of the chicken and lettuce leaves on the plates before us at the table between the windows. "Why should you object so? I don't understand. I need a little extra – for clothes and household things and food for the dog."

I rub Frère's shaggy head, which is close to my knee. On hearing Risto's loud voice, he has come to sit beside me, his yearning eyes like two half-moons.

"Because I don't want you to. Does that mean nothing? I want you to be able to be with me when it is possible for me to be free…I should say, to escape," he says angrily. "Think what I'm used to with Rose. I'm married to a ballet dancer! 8:00 o'clock in the morning, it's off to class." He is growing angrier by the moment.

"It's a religion with her. It comes first on her list of priorities, except for the performance itself. Roberto's in second place, and I guess I come in third. I'm sick of her schedules. I'm an artist! It's the same for her with love," he says with sarcasm. "Let's get it over with. Here we go with another measured teaspoon!'"

Seeing my look of horror, he stops abruptly, and coming round to my side of the table, pushes Frère aside and embraces me.

"Ah, Cammy, Cammy, forgive me. That was brutally thoughtless. But it only shows how much I need you, your spontaneity, your availability to me. Why do you think I put you so close to me? I get such longings, even from just across the street. All I want to do is run right over here and bury myself in you."

I have risen and am silently collecting the dinner dishes.

"Say something, Cammy. Are you trying to punish me with your silence? And stop fooling around with the dishes, like a child busy with her blocks."

"I am not a child," I reply coldly.

"But you are, my dear, in so many ways."

"Have I merely gone from one father to another?"

"Hardly…but speaking of your father, he'd be outraged at the idea of your working. For different reasons, of course. Camille with a job? It is not genteel." Risto stretched out the last word.

"Are you coupling yourself with my parents – against me?"

"Of course not. I'm only saying at this point in your life, why would you need to work. I can manage a little more money. I need you to be there for me, don't you understand?" He approaches me as I stand by the sink.

The evening is spoiled. I refuse any intimacy for the first time. Long after he has taken a sullen departure, I find myself eating the leftover, wilted salad in the kitchen at dawn, watching the sky grow pale over the chimney pots through the tiny kitchen window, and more determined than ever to work for Monsieur Héberd.

"I am not a child," I whisper fiercely to the dawn.

1928 Spring – Summer Paris

AND SO I LIVE

12.

AND SO I LIVE at 44, rue La Boëtie, busy with my five-hour day job at Héberd's, and occupied with my affectionate Frère. And so I love at 44, rue La Boëtie, consumed by my passion for Risto. It seems I have lived this way a long time. My lover is always caught in a whirlwind of activity, but somehow, he includes me in this maelstrom, and in spite of the woman and child across the street, we dwell circumscribed by love.

Risto is a huge success as an artist, hailed as the "Protean creator of rue la Boëtie," by a well-known critic who reviews in Le Journal. Risto's latest works are on exhibit at Vollard's on rue Lafitte in the spring of 1928. I ask Risto what "Protean" means and he explains proudly it refers to the god, Proteus, who could assume different forms.

"In other words, variable, versatile, and prophetic," he says with his extraordinary smile.

The critic is right! Risto is Protean. He is now learning metal welding from a man named Gonzalez, whom he had known from his Barcelona days and goes regularly to the man's studio on rue de Medeah.

Risto is creating lithographs as well, and wire construction, magazine covers, theater costumes, modeling in clay, painting in oil, engraving, charcoal and pencil drawing.

"Taste, taste, always taste," the Le Journal critic continues in his article. "Risto can do anything, succeeds at all he undertakes."

I am particularly excited by the review because Still Life is one of the 18 works receiving such acclaim and, of course, Still Life is my portrait in disguise, the first painting Risto ever did of me. I can laugh now at my horrified reaction and the flood of tears that followed my first vision of those colorful, separated globs and torso-like geometrics, because now people seem to find the painting wonderful.

I am not allowed to attend the opening at Vollard's. Rose will accompany Risto, but I manage to see the exhibition alone, one late afternoon at the beginning of May. I walk to rue Lafitte by a long, circuitous route through the Bois. I take advantage of the mild weather and the smells of the earth, the neat beds of sweet marguerites and early anemones in brilliant shades of purple and red. The white *fleur de lis* are deep in green gullies and birds twitter in anticipation of a summer sun.

The gallery is crowded. People are reverential, hushed. The paintings and sculptures, including Head of a Girl, are overwhelming. They are expressions from Risto's soul.

Not all the critics are so kind as Le Journal's.

A famous gentleman critic and dealer who lives in Italy is in Paris at this time to buy for his personal collection. He writes that although he always thought highly of Risto's early work, comparing his draftsmanship to Raphael's, he is repelled by Risto's new 'twists and turns of style because they teach nothing about nature'. He calls him an 'acrobat' with the personality of a 'demagogue' and claims Risto 'has done more in these postwar years to corrupt art than anyone in history'. This diatribe in Paris Soir, the evening newspaper, bothers Risto not in the least.

"Snobbish old fogie," he says, crumpling the paper and tossing it into the nearest waste basket.

One ashy spring day, I am in the office at Héberd's, working on our catalogue file, and hearing the tinkle of the front doorbell, emerge to face a striking, dark haired woman in brown coat with black stockings covering the knotty calves of her long legs. It is Rose and I freeze. Is this the moment of confrontation I have so often fantasized, where I say in haughty tones: 'Let him go. He loves only me'! and she dissolves in tears, although usually in my dream, she has Roberto clutched to the brown coat.

The meeting is no such drama. She merely wants a special edition of the book for "Parade" a ballet in which she had performed for the Ballets Russes, under the direction of the great impresario, Sergei Diaghilev, more than 10 years earlier. She requests this in nasal tomes, looking down the aquiline nose, blinking fine, dark eyes to accustom herself to the dimness.

I manage to find the volume with trembling hands, only to discover the design on the thick, parchment binder, is one of Risto's.

We finish the transaction with little conversation, and if there is any sign of acknowledgement of my true presence in Risto's life – and by connection – in her own, I see none.

Risto is angry when I tell him of the encounter that evening. "Why would Rose want a copy of "Parade"? Good God, that's the year I met her."

"Did you meet through working on the ballet?" It is the first such question I have ever asked of Risto, and it is accompanied by a nasty vision of the two, collaborating over the cover design, the beautiful dancer leaning seductively close.

"Yes, damn it, but I do not like her meeting you! If you hadn't had that job, it would never have happened."

"It could happen anywhere. We do live on the same street."

"This meeting was just too close for comfort."

"You put me here. Besides she certainly gave no sign at all of knowing who I am."

"Humph. She knows nothing. I've been careful," but he continues to regard me reproachfully as if the incident were my fault. "I warned you that job would be trouble."

Both of us are disturbed and spend a restless evening. I try to cajole him with a mainstay distraction – other than the bed – namely food. Risto does not seem interested in my poetry "Words bore me. Give me paint or a charcoal stick and a piece of paper – but not, for God's sake, little black words."

But he does love food and wine and is a chef in his own right, particularly in the making of the fish soup, *bourride*, from the south, velvet smooth and laced with garlic. Sometimes he would drop in a poached egg and powder it with cheese. Or he would concoct a peasant dish of dark red beans, rich with the flavor of sausage. "Reminds me of Barcelona," he would mutter.

The red beans are hard to find in Paris, but one can always get the *flageolet*, the small white bean with a more delicate flavor. I keep a supply in the cupboard of the little kitchen and to bring him round at this moment, I put on a pot with a lamb shank, garlic and a bit of chopped tomato.

"Here, Cammy, you must sauté the garlic first and brown the meat. The tomato can go in raw," he says with a flourish.

The aroma soon fills the small apartment so deliciously, it lulls him into a smile and knocks out the smell of clay completely. He is still working on the Head series, modeled after me.

As we eat the heavy dish washed down with red wine and morsels of bread, Risto speaks of the summer which is fast approaching.

"Dinard this year. Rose loves it, and Roberto...I can teach him to fish a little."

"Dinard?"

"I know it's where your parents go, but I thought I could find an apartment for you near the villa I have rented on the Avenue des Roches. We could arrange to be there when they are not."

"But Risto, I can't show my face in that town. I've been there too many times. I wouldn't dare go outside," I say miserably. "Must it be Dinard?"

"That's where 'they' want to go. And, my darling, I am trying to please 'them'. Rose has been acting strange lately – constantly nagging at me about my hours. She still doesn't understand I'm an artist!"

"What about Héberd's? I want to keep my job."

"There we go with that job again," he says with annoyance.

"I know, but I need it. Besides I love it. He's a dear old man and the atmosphere, oh, I don't know. It's where I want to be. And what about Frère?"

"Bring him," he says, scraping up the last beans with his bread. "Now that it's settled, come here."

But I do not 'come here'. Instead I stand before him in bewilderment. Has he heard nothing I've said? Doesn't he know how painful Dinard would be for me?

But how can he know my memories? And as firmly as he is determined I go to Dinard, just as firmly I refuse.

The last evening before Risto leaves for Dinard with his family is spent in a turmoil of sensuality against the flickering candles in the rosy bed. Finally, shadow-eyed in the morning after his departure, I go to my new percolator, another gift from Risto, to prepare black coffee loaded with sugar. On lifting the top, I see in the empty metal basket that holds the coffee, a folded piece of paper.

"Cammy, you are everything."

1928-29 Paris

THE DREAM

13.

IT IS A HUMID month of August I spend alone in Paris. I did not go to Dinard with Risto. Just what kind of holiday would it have been with the continuation of proximity to his 'family'?

The separation is a good thing. I have Frère for companionship, Monsieur Héberd for sustenance, and my notebook in which to pour out my feelings. I receive letters from Dinard on blue paper with Risto's square handwriting. From a man who does not like 'little black words', they are filled with longing. He complains of Rose, her nagging, her restlessness; 'without her damned schedule, she is impossible…always on me for something.'

The last of his letters comes at the end of August.

He grumbles about Rose, even quoting her demands. 'It's drafty! Get my wrap.' He's unable to work. 'I can't lift my hand to paint,' and he is frantically bored. His final words are startling 'When I am with the one, I think only of the other. She will never divorce me!'

Divorce! It has never occurred to me. The letter arrives shortly after I have written a poem entitled 'The Other Woman', which irony does not escape me.

Yet, during this month of August, the time is not lost. From my meager earnings, I replenish my wardrobe and splurge on lingerie of white Chantilly lace, a slip in peach satin and underpants with more lace, this time black. I buy a cherry dress of poplin and a white mohair shawl. Fall is approaching, bringing pleasure in the turning leaves, the carpets of pine needles, the musty, mushroomy smell under the old mulberry trees cut into umbrella shapes. I cannot wait for autumn. I cannot wait for Risto.

During these hot Paris days, I decide to present my poetry to Monsieur Héberd. It is at his request.

"These are remarkable, Camille," he says returning the two notebooks I have given him. "You must continue." He regards me like a sorcerer, knowing my secrets. Monsieur Héberd has never questioned me about my 'position' or my private life, but I sense he knows, although exactly who my 'Monsieur' might be, I don't think he realizes.

"Did you ever hear of a poet named Rainer Maria Rilke?"

I shake my head.

"He was an Austrian poet, born in Prague, who was so sensitive he died from the thorn prick of a rose only a year or so ago. Don't know whether or not it's true about the rose." The old man pauses to sip his coffee.

"He wrote a wonderful little book called 'Letters to a Young Poet'... among other things, I know it's here somewhere...and a monograph on the sculptor, Rodin."

"Rodin!"

"You really must read them."

We are sitting in the back office of the store. He is behind the old desk, strewn with papers – orders for books, receipts, file cards ready for the catalogue drawer. Our coffee is lukewarm, having been brewed some time ago on the adjacent grill. I am eager to read Rilke. Suddenly, I hear the tinkle of the front bell, and entering the shop from the rear office with eyes unaccustomed to the dimness, I see a chic young woman in a hat of parrot colors, with ferret teeth gleaming and lashes batting against the shadowy light.

"Zelle? It's you," I say embracing her.

"Oh, Camille, it's been ages, Can you run out for lunch? I have such news!"

The next thing I know we are in the bistro on the corner, ordering glasses of the house wine from the zinc bar, and small loaves filled with ham from the Ardennes with stone-ground mustard.

"I had a devil of a time finding you at your job…stopped by the house on Victor Hugo. Your mother said she doesn't see you much. She knew nothing of your working. You know, they didn't leave Paris at all this summer." Suzelle pauses. "Your father…he's not well."

My heart sinks and I feel lost in the noise of the busy bistro. There are a group of workmen at the zinc bar, downing their noon cognac, and buzzing like animated flies.

"They don't wish to see me. They don't approve."

Suzelle, ever sensitive, sees my distress. "Anyway, I stopped by your concierge and she said you were right down the street at Héberd's, and so you were!" The ferret teeth sparkle. She breaks some of the bread away, leaving it on her plate, and takes a bite of the pink ham. Chewing slowly, she laughs nervously.

"I have extraordinary news. It's Roger. Roger and me. We are to be married in the early winter. Right after Christmas."

"Oh, Zelle," is all I can say. I reach out and squeeze her plump hand on the table between us.

"He is adorable and we are buying a house in Neuilly. I have so many ideas for fixing it up…lots of sky blue velvet" – trust Zelle to want velvet! –"on chairs and loveseat and blue voile at the windows."

"What will be your new name?"

"LaBouchère…Madame Roger de LaBouchère…Suzelle de LaBouchère. Isn't that pretty?"

She continues chattering animatedly. I feel diminished. She is my best friend – my only friend – and I should be elated at her happiness. I am not.

We order stewed pears flavored with vanilla bean, and she looks at me with a compassion that makes me uncomfortable.

"I just wanted you to know. It's to be a tiny wedding…just family…"

I am not to be invited.

Out on the humid street, we face each other. With a tilt of the parrot-colored hat, she hugs me, looks in my eyes deeply, as if something is ending and says: "Your Maman told me to tell you she loves you."

I watch her, walking trimly up the summer street, eagerly rushing to her love.

Oh, Risto, Risto...please come home.

I return to the shop in morbid mood, stung by the contrast I see in Suzelle's and my own life. Maman has stayed in Paris in all this heat, through this long summer, and Papa?

My heart shrivels at the thought of him. Only the two books by Rilke, Monsieur Héberd has in hand for me break the despond, and I clutch them to my breast like lost treasures.

Risto finally returns. He comes back in September, a few days earlier than Rose and Roberto.

"I could stand no more of it without you!"

Although he stays in my apartment these few days, at the moment we are in his studio after making love on the flowered divan. He is brown from the sun and healthy beyond compare, his stocky body firm and muscular, pouring energy.

Risto had written he had not been able to work without me, yet he has done any number of pictures. They are not of the ocean or of Dinard or of Roberto. They are of Rose. Every one!

In them she is ugly. There is one oil showing a savage female head with voracious jaws and teeth. The head is imposed against a classic, noble profile...Risto's own.

"I call it Self-Portrait with Female."

"I don't know what to make of it."

"She buzzes in my head, yapping at me between clenched teeth. I told you I couldn't stand it any more."

There are other pictures by the dozen, containing similarly aggressive women; a head with praying mantis jaws, a woman with spike-like teeth. They are not pretty pictures, but they carry great impact.

"What does Rose think of these?"

"She didn't even look at them. She didn't have to pose for me. It's all engraved in my head. But, enough of that. I am sick of these mean-bitch pictures. I've been doing them, all six weeks, by the sea in Dinar. Now, I want to do a series of my love. I am going to call it The Dream and it will be you. There will be flowers and mirrors – you will be nude and beautiful and shaped like the petal of a flower." He looks at me intensely. "Come, let's get at it, but first…"

He pulls me to him and I sink beneath him, amazed I can so soon again respond with ardor enough to match his own.

The next months, Risto paints me nude on his couch, which he changes from a floral pattern to black in the pictures; half-nude in a chair; nude and sleeping with a mirror behind me, a double image, reflected as a mound, with a long tendril of hair. I am all egg shapes and flowing contours, with black tracery delineating the image, echoed by philodendron leaves.

"The pure mistress," he would say, heaving behind the easel. "You are my own woman."

Risto paints rapidly. He does as many as three pictures in as many days. At the studio, he paints me sitting in a chair, with a book open in my lap, one breast exposed. He paints me in the plum-colored armchair in my own salon and suddenly, I become more abstract in the pictures.

"Am I back in disguise?" I ask.

"No, No, You are the essence of mistress! You have a mythic quality…a symbol of light. You are my finest work," he exclaims.

If, as Risto says, a man's work is his autobiography, then I am surely his greatest love. The Dream paintings are lusher than any he has ever done. Occasionally, like a split personality – a see-saw – he paints Rose, in between the pictures of me. Although I have seen earlier portraits of her where she is stiffly beautiful, in the new paintings, Risto laces her persona with venom.

It disconcerts me little as the winter of 1929 arrives bitter cold, so warm is number 44 on the third floor, and number 23 in the garden studio. It is a winter filled with fervent enthusiasms, the monster bed, bouncy divan, Frère, bookstore, ardent lover, smells of oil, paint, turpentine, grilling sole, and *Roquefort* cheese – and especial warmth in a new, fur-lined hood Risto gives me.

Spring follows, more rainy and chill than usual, but who notices?

And summer next. Risto starts a new series of lyrical, erotic engravings of me that he produces for months. He has shipped Rose and his son off to Juan-Les-Pins in the south for the month of August, so we are alone together in Paris.

One day mid-summer, he turns to me and says, “How would you like your portraits to go to New York, Cammy, eh? Did you know a new Museum of Modern Art is opening in New York in November of this year? It’s a very important event. There’s lots of money behind it. They’ve already contacted me. There is to be a special exhibition in January called ‘Painting in Paris’, and they want some of my works.”

Risto waves a thin, airmail envelope at me. He is obviously excited.

“A man will come around to select what will be sent. The first American exhibition for me…but not the last, by God! Eh, Cammy? They will be coming off Park Avenue by the hundreds to take a look at my girl!”

And it happens…not the hundreds of people coming off Park Avenue to look at me, but 14 of his works are shipped to New York, including two unrecognizable Dream versions of myself. From the Museum of Modern Art, after a big, if mixed, success, they are sent to the Reinhardt Gallery, in that enormous American city, New York, and from thence to a showing in Chicago.

As the year 1929 runs out, Risto is working at full tilt at every medium known to the world of art, even wood engraving, plaster, copperplate, and whittling! And he continues The Dream. It is a theme through all his work, and there, of course, am I, unfaltering, as consumed by him as ever. The culmination of the series is a large oil Risto claims is his favorite of all time.

He calls the painting Dream Entrance, in vibrant color with heavy black lines like the leadings in a stained glass window. It is of a girl, me, facing a mirror.

Risto says ‘it is the mirror of your own mortality’. But in my perception, from a distance, the center line of the mirror in the huge picture, which splits the two-dimensional surface in half, looks most disturbingly to be what lies between a woman’s legs, hidden between her thighs. The picture, like shattered glass, reflects the entrance to love itself.

Dream Entrance! It is a vision of me that is disguised beyond recognition. I know Risto means the painting to be universal. I know, from what he has said, that this part of a woman is 'where the world begins', but, oh blessed disguise!

I thank God that no one will know the painting is of me.

Part Two

1933 July Cannes

IN BONNARD'S GARDEN

14.

LITTLE HAS CHANGED. IT is the summer of 1933, a dazzline Sunday in late July, and Risto and I drive to Le Bosquet – The Grove – home of Pierre Bonnard for lunch. The house is not far from Cannes at the small town of Le Gannet, and using an open, tub of a car, Risto's new Hispano-Suiza, with its blonde basketry sides, we meander through the treacherous hills, dotted with green cypress trees, beside fields jeweled with yellow flowers. Outside the city of Cannes, the car causes considerable comment from people on the roadside.

Risto is in fine mood as we drive in the July sunlight, laughing and chattering of the past year's triumphs, exhibitions at Paul Rosenberg's, Galerie Pierre, Galerie Goëmans, and at Georges Petit's.

"There were 236 works of mine shown at Petit's alone. Formidable!" he exclaims, tooting at a lazy duck crossing the road. "I even got to London! '30 years of Risto'."

I am quiet, saying little, viewing the roadside inns we pass, brilliant with rose-flowered vines. We pause for a *verre* at a village wine shop with reddish sand where wine has spilled and there is a dank coolness.

I had arrived in Cannes by train from Paris two days earlier. Risto has taken a villa for the month. He occupies it with Rose and Roberto.

He has booked a room for me for the weekend at a small pension, L'Auberge du Citronnier, an inn named for the lemon tree in its tiny courtyard, not far from Risto's villa. My room has a balcony overlooking the sweet smelling tree, filling it with the scent of summer. The inn itself has saffron walls and blue shutters, plastered beams and Provençal tiles. There is a rose every morning in a china bud vase with my morning *café au lait.*

It is not my best judgement to come here, but Risto's letters to 44, rue La Boëtie have been of persuasive longing. I took the train two days ago, and am now at his side in this wondrous motor car, open to the wind, hair blowing, alive with sexuality after two nights of lovemaking. In the early morning, we almost merge in our sleep. I do not ask myself what Rose must think of his absence from the villa.

Risto is speaking of Pierre Bonnard, preparing me for the stranger I am to meet, drawing me back to the moment.

"...can paint anywhere; a hotel room, a guest room. His own room has only a bare light bulb and his canvases are thumbtacked to a wall with flowered wallpaper. It's a wonder he can see anything!"

"Amazing," I mumble.

"He's always painting his wife, Marthe. He married her in 1925 – after 30 years of living together! Strange one, that Marthe. Sort of reclusive." Risto gives a harsh little laugh. "Wonder if she'll have lunch with us."

Risto tells me how Bonnard paints Marthe just as she was when he met her, a 16-year-old midinette he had to possess.

"She went by the fancy name of Marthe de Meligny – not her real name, of course – as if she were a *cocotte.* He paints her ageless, a memory of passion. He's like a Peeping Tom, tiptoeing into her toilette, then rushing to his room to recreate the memory. He paints her in her bath like a water lily so he can diffuse the light and hide the aging signs, the wattles and wrinkles. The man loves her enough to keep her perennially young. Anyway, he's a sweet man!"

We are turning into a driveway of pounded dirt by a series of luxuriant flowerbeds with blooms of lavender and blue and orange. The house is a fieldstone structure, probably once a farmer's cottage. It is set in a clump of shadowy trees. The front door is open with a small man standing at the entrance.

It is Monsieur Bonnard. He hardly looks an artist...more like one of the accountants who worked at my father's insurance firm. Wiry, dapper in his printed ascot, wearing steel-rimmed glasses and a small moustache, I am unprepared for the smile of a Paris *gamin*, with even white teeth and a bubbling good humor behind the smile.

"Come in. Come in, my dear Risto – and what a charming Mademoiselle. Camille, isn't it?"

I am flattered Risto has made him aware of my existence and of my name.

"It IS Camille, Monsieur Bonnard. Thank you for including me."

"Welcome to Le Bosquet, my retreat. I bought it the year I married. It's my pride."

With these remarks, two large, oldish dogs make their wagging appearance, greeting us at the door with their master. The black Labrador seems to be smiling.

"Ubu, Mademoiselle Camille – and of course, you know Risto – and Pucette." Pucette, Little Flea. Come through to the garden. We'll lunch outside."

We enter a hallway and go into a charming salon with wallpaper covered in tiny flowers. Hung upon the walls are paintings, all by our host; the nude Marthe in several of them; a dining room, the replica of the one we are about to enter, with glass doors open to a garden beyond and distant field; indoor-outdoor landscapes of perennial summer, filled with sunlight and flowers; a canvas of a table set with homely objects, a wine carafe, a plain ceramic pitcher, a vase of flowers, a tart tin right from the kitchen, their simplicity grounding the mass of color.

One painting draws my attention in particular. It is called Le Cabinet de Toilette. Of extraordinary color, yellow-rose light, and feminine jumble, the nude body is bathed in an ethereal tint, tilted forward, one firm, young breast defined in white.

"This interests you? I painted it only last year. Do you like it?"

"Ah, yes," I respond, but I am really thinking more of the fact that Marthe must be a woman in her mid-fifties. In the painting, she looks to be half that age. I wonder too how Monsieur Bonnard managed to catch her in this pose. Just as Risto had said. he must have tiptoed around and peeked at her.

If the living room is a jumble of brilliant color and objects, the dining room, with its polished wooden walls, doors open to the outside, is a serene contrast. Simple, with straight, provincial furniture, the room only asks to be passed through to the breathtaking garden and a gentle meadow beyond.

Under a cluster of cypress trees is set an inviting table, covered with white cloth and thick, white china. There are places for four. Pouring three glasses of local white wine from a chilled carafe, we sit in three of the chairs around the table, as the dogs cavort on the thick grass at our feet, Ubu rolling luxuriously on his back. The fourth glass – Marthe's glass – awaits her, empty.

Risto and Monsieur Bonnard are talking art with animation. "You know, Pierre, my old canvases come back to haunt, like prodigal sons – but they return home to me wearing shirts of gold."

"I'm glad for you," replies our host. "But, tell me what you're doing new? Controversial? – for you are certainly that, my friend."

"Well, I'm beginning to work with all sorts of ordinary objects. A colander – a real one becomes a human head…so much for brains, eh?" Risto laughs.

"What an idea!"

Risto, warming to Monsieur Bonnard's obvious interest, continues.

"Or a faucet, an old lock, a wrench, a simple smoking pipe, each becomes the center of a sculpture or collage. I made a fantastic horned bull's head out of a bicycle seat, the seat – the snout – the handlebars – the horns." Risto's hands are outlining his thought.

"My word!"

"The bull's head is a marvel!" Risto then begins to speak of his latest project in Paris, the cover he has done for the first issue of a new magazine, Minotaur.

"I made a collage on a piece of wood, tacking pasteboard first to it, on top of which I put an engraving of a minotaur, surrounded the beast with ribbons and faded artificial flowers from one of Rose's hats."

I nearly choke on my wine. Must he mention her here?

Monsieur Bonnard shoots me a clearly sympathetic glance.

"Ah, my dear Marthe – we're waiting for you," he says suddenly, rising to his feet.

I turn, and through the glass doors, Marthe glides. In a dress reaching to the ground, also covered with flowers like the wallpaper, Marthe Bonnard comes to the table without a smile on the round, childish face. Her eyes are distant.

She is a small woman and does look younger than her years, although she is obviously middle aged and certainly not so young as the woman in Le Cabinet de Toilette. She has an air of being preserved like a butterfly. She offers no hand – not even a limp one – in greeting, just sits at table.

Monsieur Bonnard proffers her filled wine glass and commences to pass the large platter brought by the cook, laden with plump mussels in a lemony vinaigrette, a salad of soft lettuce leaves with fresh basil, and a loaf of newly baked bread. It is a delectable meal under the swaying cypress trees, with Risto and Monsieur Bonnard holding forth on painting and collage and etching with enthusiasm. Marthe says not one word. Nor do I.

I shyly glance beneath lowered eyelids at her face. She eats silently, a neurasthenic pallor glazing her skin. The rounded lips open for tiny bites. Behaving as if no one is there, she folds her napkin and leaves her place at the table.

"No dessert, Marthe? Cook made a fresh peach *tarte*," Monsieur Bonnard protests, again rising to his feet. But Marthe merely gives a negative shake of her head and glides through the glass dining room doors into the house. Monsieur Bonnard's face reflects a pained disappointment. His obvious sadness touches me, and I feel an affinity with him I do not understand.

Risto is talking obliviously. "Next week, I leave for Barcelona. My old stamping grounds, where I learned in my teens the seamy side of the streets. Those were the hot-blooded days...received my instruction from the kind young prostitutes. There's something especially exciting about a port city!"

"You're going to Barcelona?" I ask in astonishment, alarmed at the idea of such separation. Risto's being in a foreign country I cannot even visualize seems threatening. "For how long? Is the trip because of the new magazine?"

"No, no, Cammy. It is just a jaunt into old memory." Then, turning to Bonnard, he says, "I want to take Roberto to the Barcelona Museum. They recently acquired a collection of my works from those days, and I want the boy to see what his Papa is capable of. Some of the work may be beyond him, if you know what I mean." Risto gives a lecherous little laugh. "But it's time for Roberto to know what I do, that I'm famous!" He slaps his knee.

Monsieur Bonnard, flushed with something akin to embarrassment, is cutting the shimmering *tarte* into wedges. It is served in the fluted tin in which it was baked.

Hearing Risto's plans and his speaking of Roberto whom he rarely discusses with me has been a cold shock. To gain self-control, I concentrate on the greedy, brown eyes of Ubu. His head reaches almost to the tabletop, and his covetous eyes are riveted on the peach *tarte.*

Monsieur Bonnard puts a wedge of *tarte* on each of three plates – the fourth remains forlornly bare – places a large dollop of *crème fraiche* beside each piece and serves each of us

"Yes, I thought I would drive with Rose and Roberto in the new car. We'll go through Perpignan and down the Costa Brava to Sitges, and from there it's nothing to Barcelona. What a wild and craggy coast it is! We'll stay at the Ritz Hotel in Barcelona. It's not often I unloose the purse strings, but I am in the mood to enjoy."

Risto is devouring his *tarte.* I cannot swallow, for what I have just sampled has turned to ashes in my mouth.

1933 July – October Paris

"RISTO ET SES AMOURS"

15.

Le Train Bleu is aptly named for the wretched journey I take back to Paris. It is hot and crowded with returning weekenders, and my mood is green with jealousy. All I can think of is the gay threesome heading for Perpignan and Barcelona.

I endure the night in disquiet. The train passes slowly through stations where a lantern jerks in the darkness swinging from a wooden arm, or a man is seen pushing a trunk on a handcart with sleepy steps.

Does he love me? I have never doubted it before. How can he go off on a lighthearted adventure – to the Ritz Hotel, of all glamorous places – with the shrike of a woman he claims not to be able to stand? Is it just for Roberto? Or is the trip just for his own recollections of hot nights in Barcelona? or perhaps to see again the cruel sport of bull-fighting which has always fascinated him?

Where does all this leave me?

Risto and I have been together for six years. The equilibrium of the two of us has never been truly shaken but my balance, this dark night on the Blue Train, is upset by Risto's insouciant journey to Spain.

Today, this Sunday – is it the same day? It feels like a different day entirely. Monsieur Bonnard's warmth had softened me.

"You and I will be friends," Bonnard had said to me as Risto and I had taken our departure. "I feel it. Friends, always!" and with that, he had leaned over and kissed me on the cheek.

This day had started with a morning swim off the empty beach in Cannes not far from L'Auberge du Citronnier before driving to Le Gannet and our luncheon *chez* Bonnard. It was early, the sky a gentle French blue, with pink along the horizon and a sea the color of aquamarines. I am a strong swimmer from my summers at Dinard, as is Risto, and we made our way with easy crawl through the rippling water to a wooden raft not far from the shore.

There we had made slithery love, under the open sky, I could hear a cock crowing and the sound of geese, the bird-voices drifting from the shore as Risto took me in leisurely strokes, almost as if we were still swimming. We were as two creatures from the sea that have climbed atop a rock to love in the sun.

We lay there in the soft air, skin tasting of salt from the sea, the wind freshening about us, a beautiful way to begin any day. Risto sat up after moments and said:

"Look, Cammy. Look at La Croisette," and he pointed to the elegant promenade separating the beach from the great hotels in Cannes. "See the ring of hills behind it? Someday, I'm going to line La Croisette and those hills with elephantine sculptures facing the sea, like the mysterious figures of Easter Island. No one knows how they got there, you know. Someday, they will wonder just that of my sculptures. What magician put them there?"

Risto's eyes were burning as he described his vision. Finally, he lay back next to me.

"I have already done the pen and ink drawings. It took me years to draw like a child. Finally I do. The drawings are so...so...elemental." Then, smiling, he said, "They will be a self-tribute."

"Do you think the city fathers will let you do such a thing?"

"Why not? I'm their most celebrated visitor...their favorite son."

"Will they be beautiful statues?"

"Don't say 'statues'. They will be enormous, imposing, vital figures. Yes, and beautiful, of course. More monumental than Modigliani's caryatids, and much larger." He paused. "This isn't a new idea. It's been a long-time dream."

So saying, he dove into the sea. I followed, startled by his need for self-tribute. We had reached the beach, now lightly peopled with bathers in rubber swimming shoes so as not to cut their feet on the stones.

As I had emerged from the water, Risto watched me closely. My hair was dripping. The wet suit outlined my breasts and hips. I had felt young, as supple and taut as only the young can be. He came toward me.

"Cammy, you are one such figure. I wish I could put you on a hill behind Cannes for all the world to see. You'd be most elemental of all!"

And we were off to Monsieur Bonnard's, stopping on the way to change clothes, and later at the wine shop on the road to Le Gannet to down a brandy for I was chilled from the swim and the open car.

That was this morning. Was it really this morning? The day progressed happily enough until the peach *tarte*, which I could not swallow because Risto was going away for a special holiday with his 'family'.

The return from lunch to L'Auberge du Citronnier in the Hispano-Suiza motor, after bidding farewell to the solitary figure of Monsieur Bonnard, was passed in silence. From the inn, after gathering up my things from the room with the balcony, we had gone to the terrace at Basso's. Sitting there in the breeze from the sea, I awaited the severing of the string, which twined us together at this moment, the thread of physical presence that would be broken by my departure.

Now, on the *Train Bleu*, I am a thundercloud. The hostility is in my throat, galling in its acridity. There is always Rose! She is a fact of life. There is always the boy as well. Like two of the elemental figures Risto plans to erect to line La Croisette and stand on the hills of Cannes, they are rooted to his earth.

I pass the summer listlessly with Risto finally returning to Paris from Barcelona earlier than Rose and Roberto, complaining of his boredom with them. He goes immediately to Chevauchers, a small Château near Gisors, about forty miles northwest of Paris. The Château is named for the horsemen who rode its many bridle paths. It has an enormous stable, now defunct, Risto has converted to a studio. He had purchased the country home two years ago for escape and work. I accompany him.

The first painting he produces is an oil on wood called Lady Bullfighter, an excruciating picture with an enormous bull stuck with picks and a sword, a horse in agony from the bull's horns, and a female body crumpled on the back of the beast. I am struck cold by its violence. Is the woman Rose? Or could that lady be me?

My reaction is momentarily assuaged by the gentle living, the splendid loving, and Risto's presence. But again, I must leave, carrying Frère in the back of Risto's automobile in a box. He sleeps peacefully all the way, which is more than I can say for myself, for Rose and Roberto are returning to Paris and will be joining the Pater Familias at the Château de Chevauchers.

Autumn begins at 44, rue La Boëtie in normal pattern with my job a few steps from my door, my dog at the end of an outstretched hand, and my love, returned to 23, rue La Boëtie across the street.

One fine October evening with gusts swirling the dropping leaves in the streets, the stars are cold above the City of Light. I rush to meet Risto in my fur-lined hood, at Le Petit Clos. The place has not changed. Madame La Patronne still does not pry into her customer's privacy and the chicken legs with curry sauce are as robust as ever.

We are to dine early there – as we do on occasion – and go to a special exhibition of Rodin's drawings at his temple, the Musée Rodin, around the corner from the tiny restaurant.

It is special for me, because Risto is extremely cautious. We are rarely in public together in Paris, but I have cajoled him into attending this exhibition with me.

"You know you always said 'the hand is the instrument of magic'," I expounded. " Who sculpted hands better than Rodin? You must see them again."

"Why not?" Risto had said, finally capitulating.

Now, I rush through the bracing night as if walking on the stars themselves and find myself alone at a pink-linen covered table at Le Petit Clos. I do not wait long before Risto arrives in a flurry of overcoat, a scowl on his face deepening the lines that bracket his mouth like a parenthesis.

"Sorry to keep you waiting," he mumbles, throwing himself down on the opposite chair.

"You are in a state," I proclaim.

"You couldn't be more right," he says, clamping his lips shut. He orders wine for us both and sits in stony silence until the glasses are brought.

"Have I done something to make you angry?"

"Of course not! Why must you think it would have to be something you did or said?" he says so abruptly, I flush.

"Forgive me, Cammy." He reaches for my hand. "I am in a state and it has nothing to do with you."

"Is it Rose?"

"She's not the instigator, but she's upset, and when she's upset, she makes my life a hell!"

"What is it?" I ask, mystified.

"Some very adverse...er...publicity that has just been published about me. A pack of lies! An outrage." His face reddens

"Drink your wine and calm down," I say. "Please." He takes a sip, then another.

"Damn!"

"What kind of publicity?" I ask.

"A book."

"A book?"

"Yes, a book. 'Risto et ses Amours'."

"You're joking."

"I wish I were."

It is I who takes a large gulp of wine. "Am I...am I in it?"

"Of course not," he exclaims. "Why must you always think everything has to do with you!"

I color. I find his response odd. Am I not one of his *amours*? Am I not the *amour* of his life? "Who wrote it?" I finally ask.

"A bitch named Justine Dupin."

"And who is she?"

"Just a woman I knew," he says under his breath.

"Just a woman you knew?"

"I knew her very well." There is a long silence.

"Is there any way to stop its publication?" I ask.

"Too late," he says, sullenly. "I've already tried but now the damn thing is out...in the book shops." And Risto bangs a fist on the table.

"I'd like to read this book," I say softly, eyeing him.

"Not on your life! It would only make you wonder about me. It's more than I can stand that Rose has read it. It's a bunch of garbage but Rose believes it – every word. She made such a scene, I almost couldn't meet you. She threatened to kill herself, can you imagine? Of course, she won't, but then she threatened to leave and take Roberto with her. Just let her try. He's my son!"

I am taken aback by his vehemence.

"I want to read it."

"Absolutely not...and why? Why would you want to read a lurid account of my earlier life which has nothing to do with you?"

"Why should Rose be so upset? Does it have something to do with her?"

"It's stuff about women in my life after she and I were married."

"After you were married?" I am shocked. "Why are you so angry if it's a pack of lies?" I pursue.

"Because Rose believes it!"

"To hell with Rose!"

"Cammy!" He looks at me askance. "It's very easy for you to say that...you forget I have a son."

"You forget it often enough." I can't help myself.

"That does it! I don't believe this."

"You don't get angry on my behalf. Oh no. It's not me you're protecting. It's that other woman, the one before me. It's Rose you're shielding."

"And why not. This has absolutely nothing to do with you."

Angrily I stuff down a nameless meal as ashen as the peach *tarte*, and we rush through the Rodin exhibit. He finally takes me to my front door and gives me a kiss as abstract as one of his paintings.

I enter the lonely apartment, dark but for a single light by the plum-colored chair. Frère greets me eagerly, but senses I am in no mood to play. I sit in the chair and make up my mind to order *'Risto Et ses Amours'* through Monsieur Héberd in the morning.

I do so the next day, stumbling in embarrassment.

"But, Camille. Why should you want to read such a book?"

"I…I'm so interested in art," I stammer.

"This, my dear, has nothing to do with art!"

Suddenly, his eyes lighten with understanding and he says no more, but orders the volume that afternoon from his supplier who stops at the shop for his monthly order, coincidentally, this very day. I have the book in hand within the week, and read it, every word, from first to last.

I wish I hadn't.

1934 August Gisors

CHÂTEAU DE CHEVAUCHERS

16.

THAT'S ME? IT HARDLY looks like a woman…with two funny legs pressed together, two nipples way up high, practically under my arm, which is curled back. I look like I have no joints! My body has been reinvented!

I look like a pillow that has just been made love to, a cushion, surrounded by flowers beside a stream, dreaming there among the reeds – with no eye or eyelid or lash or brow, my body suffused with pink – like a cloud.

The picture does not look like me – but it represents the way I feel when he loves me. How is Risto able to put my sexual feelings on canvas so accurately?

There aren't words for sexual response – only noises and shapes. A picture is better. It shows how parts of the body grow out of proportion. Feeling distorts, so why shouldn't he paint me all shifted around.

I am standing in front of the painting, entitled Nude Asleep. It is an enormous canvas, almost as tall and as long as I, propped against the white-washed stone wall of Risto's studio at his country home, the Château de Chevauchers at Gisors.

His studio is a converted room over the old stable with an attic, where once, fodder had been stored. An apple orchard stretches away from the building, through which bridle paths radiate, in the form of a star, ending in the center with an open glade. Risto does not ride, but he loves to stroll through the forest of fruit trees in the evening. Some fine days, we picnic in the glade or walk beside the nearby river L'Epte.

I am in the center of the studio, a yellow towel wrapped about my hips, breasts bare. It is 11:00 o'clock in the morning on an August day in 1934, but earlier, in a lazy dawn, I had heard a cock crowing and the sound of geese, and had drifted into a dream of Cannes and the raft and two elemental figures making love upon it.

Rose and Roberto are in Juan-Les-Pins for the month, leaving me to preside, like a young matron, at her county retreat.

The light from the countryside filters into the studio. The huge room is filled with half-finished busts in limestone and clay, heads of women, frightening African masks, as well as innumerable paintings – brilliant, cubist diagonals, organic forms, spiky shapes. There are black and white drawings of minotaurs in the act of rape, embracing women who look very much like me.

Two skeletal guitars, the only music Risto cares for, and an instrument whose structure he finds beautiful, and his collection of smoking pipes adorn the long wall to the left of the window, a window open to the *plein air*, without glass.

Among these works, we had made love last night, illuminated by candles. Risto had placed large tapers on the heads of three stonework figures of women, one candle behind an African mask, light shining through eyes and mouth in awesome manner, another flame on one of the stained tables so as to reflect in a mirror hanging on the lofty, white wall.

"Like some primitive temple!" he had exclaimed about the effect, and to me, nude in the eerie light, he said, "and you are my goddess!"

I felt my body glowing, like the pink, cushion-like figure in the picture with no sharp edges, and Risto, he was as bold with me as the minotaur in one of his drawings.

I lay beneath him, as squashed as a butterfly, trembling in the candlelight, in this pagan temple of a studio.

"When you take me like this, I can taste you in my mouth," I had said softly.

"What does it taste like?"

"Like caviar!"

That was last night!

Now it is late morning. My feet are cold on the bare floor. I rub one foot against the back of the other leg to warm it. I can hear the stirrings in the kitchen on the first floor, directly below the studio, and smell the onions Henriette, his *femme de tout faire*, is stewing in butter with a bit of nutmeg for the lunchtime *quiche* Risto and I will share.

I pick up my clothes from the evening before, scattered about the room, a long smock-like shift in brilliant blue, a pair of underpants beneath one of the paint tables, and some leather thong sandals next to the armoire. Risto had fashioned the sandals for me in polished leather and metal buckles. No bra. Risto does not like 'beauty confined'.

According to Risto, ever since Manet painted La Blonde Aux Seins Nus in 1876, a picture of a lady with bare breasts revealed from a deliberately opened bodice, the stays and corsets of European women have been loosened, never to be fully bound again. Risto believes in freedom of spirit and body.

A whistle pierces the air, and from the stone stairwell, Risto bounds into the room.

"Ah, Cammy, do you like my vision of you?" he smiles, indicating the large canvas behind me. "Or would you have preferred I paint you the way Boucher painted Louise O'Morphy, splay-legged on a couch, bottom in air? You looked so...exposed this morning, everything so visible, I couldn't resist. Was it unfair of me to paint you like this?"

I move close to him, clutching the evening smock from last night to my breast, feeling his persona so intensely, I cannot remember his face. I know that for this moment in his life at least, the painting reflects the sensation of sexual comfort he finds in making love to a particular woman. Me.

It has been all of seven years, for us, and except for his trip to Barcelona last summer with Rose and Roberto, and that dreadful book about his past by Justine Dupin last fall, there has been no crack in the stonework of our love. I shiver a little for I do not like to think of these incidents which, like smoke buried under embers, bide their time.

"Isn't it time you dressed?" Risto says. "I miss you. Come down stairs." He leaves the room, as quickly as he appeared.

I go naked to the standup lavatory at the head of the stairs and pour tepid water from a ceramic pitcher into a bowl on the washstand. It has been painted by Risto with bluntly-drawn exotic birds in purple and lime green.

I wash all over. Taking another yellow towel form a wooden rack in the stone wall of the small room, I pat myself dry. I can hear someone humming. The humming is from me. Replacing the towel, I turn to the looking glass over the washstand. Large, with a gilt rim, I study myself in it, gazing at the blond woman of twenty-five looking back at me from the other side of the mirror.

What does he see in me? I am no beauty. My nose is really too big for my face. Straight, blonde hair. The eyes are nice. Blue, but a little pale.

I inspect my profile in the mirror.

He always says he was captivated by this. I trace the line of my cheek with a forefinger. What is the word he used? Vulnerable.

Opening the door, I return to the studio room, go to the large, oaken armoire standing in the corner against the wall, and select a pink skirt, a white peasant blouse, and a scarf in lavender to tie around my waist. I dress quickly, suddenly hungry. Now, where are those sandals?

I look for them under the couch, in the corner by the armoire, when suddenly a sunbeam glints off the metal of a buckle that sits on the sill of the large window, drawing my attention. I see my leather sandals resting on the wide whitewashed stone, which overlooks the orchards below.

There is something in one of them, the sandal in the sunshine. It is a large green leaf.

Beneath the leaf I find a round yellowish crock with a red wax top. Next to it lies a silver spoon. Prying the lid from the ice-cold crock eagerly, I see the glistening, gray pearls of caviar into which I greedily dip the small silver spoon.

I learn later that afternoon, much to my chagrin, Risto is joining Rose and Roberto in Juan-Les-Pins for a return jaunt to Spain for the running of the bulls.

Risto does not know, this day in early August, that on his trip later in the month to the south of France, he will meet a young, half-Jewish Yugoslav woman named Evangeline Nouri, a fine photographer in her own right, fluent in Spanish from having lived in Seville in her early years. With a face, finely drawn like the strings of cat's cradle, Evangeline is exotic to the point that I will seem lost in passivity.

Nor do I know, as I savor the delicate pearl-gray beads of caviar, tasting the saltiness of the sea, that in the months to come, next to Evangeline, I will appear plain. Next to Evangeline, my innocence will pale.

Or so Risto will find me.

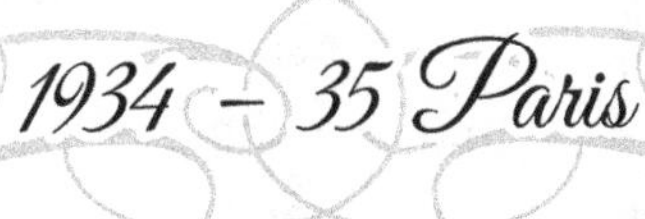

EVANGILINE

17.

It is hard to define
The line
Where dreams begin.
Goodness and sin,
Sea and sky,
Have more distinction, it seems,
Than dreams.
Walk in the mists of Paris in January.
Frost in the air obscures
All edges.

JANUARY APPROACHES, THE EIGHTH anniversary of my meeting with Risto on the frosty street in front of the windows of Galeries Lafayette where it all began. It is a lonely Noël, this December, 1934. Risto is busy paying homage to his family. Papa is so ill he is hospitalized. I have not seen him since my banishment, that afternoon in August, 1927. And Maman is preoccupied with hospital visits. I have not been there. Maman said it would only upset Papa.

My world does not feel the same. It is as if I am listening. I am here to love Risto, yet the fabric of my life seems too stretched in a direction

I cannot fathom. Sometimes, there is a closed expression on Risto's face as if it were made of *papier maché*.

The subdued Nöel passes and January too and finally, one February afternoon, with wind whipping the trees with a ferocity not usual in the streets of Paris, I make my way to Risto's studio at 23, rue La Boëtie after finishing my daily stint at Héberd's. I go there because I must, on the pretense of returning a small sketch of me reading on the old couch in my salon that he had forgotten at 44, rue La Boëtie the previous week. He will want it for the upcoming exhibition at Galerie Pierre in two days.

As I tap on the studio door, I glance around to see the reflection of Monsieur Héberd's spectacles watching me from the window of the bookshop across the street.

Risto opens the door to me, looks a bit startled, then bids me enter the familiar atelier with a nervous smile. I present him with the drawing, which I have concealed against my chest under my coat to protect it from the wind.

On the couch before me, lounging with elegant ease is a woman. She is dressed in black trousers, an uncommon sight, with cropped, dark hair and voluptuous lips with a good deal of lipstick. She is stunning, slim, casual, with long tapering fingers, tipped with red polish.

There is something indefinable in her face with its tight skin. There is money written there – or a desire for it. She looks very much at home on the flowered divan, as if she had been there often enough.

"Evangeline Nouri," Risto says. "This is Camille Ruy, one of my models and a good friend." I notice a high-pitched edge to his voice. "Evangeline is an excellent photographer and is doing a series of studies on film of my work. It is for a book of pictures that is coming out – a king of retrospective."

Evangeline nods at me with a barely perceptible smile, and I notice with some relief, a canvas camera case on the floor by her feet, shod in stylishly pointed shoes. Still, I feel outmatched.

"Ah, good," Risto continues quickly. "I am glad you brought this over. It fits right in with the sequence of Girl Dreaming, Girl Reading, Girl Drawing. Thank you, Camille."

So it's 'Camille' now? Where is the 'Cammy' of familiarity? And so, I am 'one of his models'?

"May I see the sketch, Risto?" Evangeline speaks in a low voice in strongly accented French.

He complies and she takes a thoughtful look at the drawing.

"It's beautiful...but not quite dramatic enough for the series I am photographing. Don't you think so?"

"Perhaps you're right...but I'll need it for the Pierre exhibition."

"Well, I'll leave you to your work," I interject, backing to the door, buttoning my new black coat, feeling it positively old-fashioned as compared to the chic displayed on the couch.

"Fine, fine..." says Risto. "I'll be seeing you later, eh?" he adds softly at the open door.

"I expect so," I reply vaguely. And I am gone, back to my apartment to stand in the middle of the salon, which suddenly looks sloppily overblown, the charm tarnished, the fireplace grimy, and there is dog hair on the plum-colored cushions.

"She has been working with me for some time," Risto explains to me later that evening when he arrives after dinner for a *café flitre* and a brandy.

"When did you meet?" I ask, as casually as I am able.

"Oh, last summer, in Spain. Man Ray – you've heard of the famous photographer? He brought her by the villa. She knew of my work and wanted to see it first hand. She's really quite an artist in her own way. Photography is not a fine art, of course, but it does have its purposes. She's been taking pictures of various stages as I work on one specific painting. Makes for an interesting progression, no?"

"So she has been to your studio often?"

"Quite frequently," he says.

"Is she a close...friend of Man Ray? A '*petite amie*'?"

Risto colors slightly, "I don't believe it's anything like that. She's sort of his *protégé*."

Risto fiddles with his brandy glass. "Perhaps a little more of this?" he says, offering the glass. "And enough of Mademoiselle Nouri...an interesting woman, but a bit sophisticated for my taste. I don't like the pants! Come here."

Some time later, Risto is asleep in the disordered bed. I rise, and clutching a silk robe around me, go into the salon. I am determined to avoid the thought that Risto is a traitor, ensconced under the rosy quilt, an absentee seeking the camouflage of sleep, the hidden lair that brooks no questions.

Has Risto made love to Evangeline? Do they perform on the couch of an afternoon? Has she stayed all night?

Dreadful images! More dreadful than any thought of Rose might be! I know Risto's innermost opinion of Rose. I do not know the extent of his desire for Evangeline's company or the degree of yearning for her body, a rather superb one, if a man is partial to the angular. Risto has always exclaimed with delight over my generous proportions, so I feel a small victory in being of my physical type, but the victory is short lived because Evangeline seems far more exotically beautiful than ever I could be, even if she does wear pants!

Certainly the logic of her being in the studio is most explicit, yet I know he has always despised photography as such, calling it 'sterile', 'a cold representation of life - without heart - as in art', this said with a derisive laugh.

Yet, I defend Risto. I protect him as I protect Frère on the streets against dog catchers; I protect him as I protect the books in Monsieur Héberd's book store against thieving students; I protect him as I protect this apartment on the third floor of 44, rue La Boëtie by bolting the door at night. I defend him with love in my heart because I must.

Rising at dawn, Risto joins me in the kitchen where I am preparing coffee.

"Ah, I see you have winter melon! How did you ever find such a prize," he says.

He relishes the cold fruit, and quickly swallowing his coffee, is "off on my long journey to the other side of the street!" Before he leaves, he looks about the salon and bedroom and asks, with a perfunctory kiss, "Have I left anything important this time? That drawing was necessary for the showing at Galerie Pierre. Thank you for bringing it over. But is there anything else I've forgotten? I want to save you the trip."

He is out of the apartment and down the stairs before I can respond.

If the 'long journey to the other side of the street' is only a matter of steps, why should he care that I might have to make it to deliver a forgotten belonging or necessary drawing? My suspicions only mount. They determine me to make another foray to the studio.

I have a mental picture of Risto and Evangeline so visually disturbing, my heart seems to die.

That is not all that dies this day. My father perishes at the hospital. Monsieur Héberd is waiting for me with the news at the bookstore when I finally arrive there.

He informs me of Papa's death in the most solicitous way. My knees give way, and he catches me before I fall to the ground. He sets me gently in the large chair behind his own desk. He runs to get a cup of black coffee with lots of sugar as my tears fall, deceptive tears, for I do not know what I feel.

All I know is that I must cry.

Another rubber band has snapped.

Two days later, I dress for the interment, which is to be at Père-Lachaise cemetery, in my most somber clothes. Risto is not to accompany me, begging off with the remark, "I don't want to embarrass your mother."

He is undoubtedly right, but he promises to be with me this evening.

I make my way to the burial by autobus at 4:00 o'clock this freezing February afternoon, and enter the enormous enclave of Père Lachaise on its hillside in the east of Paris.

The famed cemetery, named for the confessor of Louis XIV, was opened in 1804. Napoleon desired to be buried here, but the French instead honored him with the magnificent tomb in Les Invalides, which had originally been a disabled veterans hospital. Les Invalides. Right near the Musée Rodin.

Papa will rest in good company, with Molière, Appolinaire, Musset and Balzac beside him; Rossini and Bellini, the composers; artists

Delacroix, Corot, Modigliani. I wonder ironically if Risto will be buried here!

I pass by Chopin's grave watched over by an exquisite, sculpted muse, and along a path that passes the remains of Abélard and Heloïse. The legend of these tragic lovers created a romantic ambiance in Père Lachaise that has made it a favorite rendezvous for lovers. Papa is in the company of the talented and the brilliant and the romantic. God rest his soul. He would have approved of none of them.

There are hundreds of trees in Père Lachaise, but there are hundreds of thousands more graves and columns and mausoleums and obelisks. The view of Paris, as seen from the terrace in front of the chapel at the top of the hill, is one of the whole throbbing city. I finally find Maman and her two brothers.

I stand before the open grave with Maman, in her black cloak, and my two uncles whom I have not seen since I was a child. The two elderly men look smaller to me and considerably fatter. We say nothing to each other. The wind whips about us, flapping the dark coats each of us wears. We look like five strange birds – the priest being the fifth – on the hill top with dark feathers ruffled by the gusts.

Papa, how I wish I had known you. It is too late now. Our contretemps will always go unresolved. It will be buried with you beneath the earth, secret forever. I feel an enormous loss, as I watch the earth being shoveled over the casket hiding the few blossoms Maman has thrown upon the coffin-top. The priest mumbles in Latin and I am transported to the rocky shore of Dinard, where Papa, then a young and vigorous man, taught me to swim under water.

In Dinard, there was a rock in the middle of the cove to which we swam. To me, it seemed kilometers from land but, in reality, was perhaps a few meters, no more. Papa would ask me to hold my nose and submerge my body under the cool waves and see if I could swim to the slippery rock with its underwater coating of green lichens. I always gave up halfway, yet Papa would still reward me with a treat. He could be kind and I had loved him, but as I grew he could not accept my becoming adult. From the age of 13, he never approved of me again.

I hold Maman to me fiercely in the wind at Père Lachaise cemetery as we say goodbye. Her face is swollen with grief and fear for the lonely future. Pressing together, I hear her murmur.

"Poor, dear child. I miss you. Come soon to see me. I love you, Camille."

And Papa is gone.

In the salon of 44, rue La Boëtie, I sit huddled on the couch, caressing Frère. It is a quiet moment, the soft light of one lamp shining on the dark and curly fur of the small dog in my lap. I mourn.

And I pray, not for a future because that seems to have stopped. I pray for the past and for forgiveness, not so much from God as from Papa. Right now, they seem one and the same.

Risto does not come that night. The next morning my anxiety about him is so numbing that I drift through my morning walk with Frère and the few steps to work at Héberd's.

At lunch time, I can stand no more and go to the studio at 23, rue La Boëtie, to tap forlornly at the door. I try the latch and the door opens of itself, unusual, as Risto generally locks it. The studio is empty. My relief is enormous. I had been filled with nameless fears.

As I turn to leave, heavy with guilt as if afraid to be found in this place, which used to be a haven, I notice two paintings, side by side, against one wall.

One is a blown-up version of the sketch of me reading on the couch in my apartment. It is now a large oil. There is a window behind me, but there is no view. The window is vacant.

The other oil, exactly the same size, is of Evangeline. She is also reclining, reading on a couch in exactly the same pose. It is the flowered divan in the studio on which she lies and there is a window, too, behind her, but it is filled with leafy budding trees. Evangeline looks angular and tense but distinctly erotic.

I look at the backs of the pictures. I don't know why. They are dated the very same day. Yesterday. February 18th, 1935. One is entitled Camille Reading: the other, just Evangeline.

In the paintings, each of us is nude.

1935 June Paris

THE LETTER

18.

I AM STILL WITH RISTO. We are intimate often. None of the outer trappings are changed, but the interior life is as shifted and distorted as the first painting he ever did of me, Still Life. It is an appropriate title.

My feelings for him are no different. He still breathes life into my existence, but it is his perception of me. He is more curt. He is too busy. He is abrasive. In our lovemaking, he seems preoccupied. I have only one word for it. Evangeline!

I have ceased to go to the studio often. She is always there photographing. Risto is doing a huge painting titled War, in anticipation of a conflict in Europe he feels sure is coming, a vision of a devastated city, with animals and humans in agony. Evangeline hovers about its every stage of completion.

It has been eight years since I walked in the mists of Paris that fateful January day. Now I am behind the clouds, invisible. Risto has erased me by becoming involved with his new 'conquest', a military metaphor if ever there was one.

Then it happens that which had always been in the cards. I see the square handwriting on the blue envelope. It is addressed from across the street. The envelope feels like a flame in my hand. I gingerly unfold the fragile paper. It is a long letter for a man who does not like 'little black words'.

"Goodbye my darling little girl: This year for both of us has been a see-saw of misery. I am exhausted! Perhaps I have a small heart. Yours is enormous by comparison. You gave it to me so fully, so simply."

"What can I give you any longer? I can get no divorce from Rose, even though she has moved with Roberto to a hotel on a side street off the Champs-Elyseés. The laws of my native Spain prohibit divorce and besides, she wants everything I own. I am split in two."

(More like three! He does not mention Evangeline. So Rose has finally left him! Over Evangeline? Or me? Or both?)

"This year has been the worst time of my life. Cammy, I must be free – free to go where you cannot possibly accompany me, free to see what you cannot see. I can belong to no one. I desire all that life can provide – and some things it cannot."

"I no longer dare to love you, Camille. Don't be angry with me if I can no longer be caught up in the tentacles of the love you weave. You have consumed me in a fever of the senses, with your limpid eyes and heartfelt silences."

"You are still so young! You will find someone fresh and clean, with a future and a faith beyond any you have known with me. If you were with me now there is no way I could resist for you are incomparable – but you are not here, and I must say goodbye. R."

Chilled and trembling on this sunless morning, I move slowly across the room, bumping a small table. Frère, who has been crouched at my feet gazes at me. He turns his eyes to the door expectantly as if waiting for someone who will not come again. Don't bother to wait, dear Frère. Risto will not appear. He has rejected me, plain and simple. He chooses all that is not me.

As with the self-portrait mirror on the wall of his studio, there is a crack across my heart.

Standing by the window, I see in my mind's eye through the screen of rain the lemon tree in Cannes made silver by the moon underneath which passes the figure of the young woman, running to her lover.

Suddenly, I feel mutilated like a bird crushed beneath the wheels of a glossy Hispano-Suiza. Only then do I crumple into tears. Starting slowly from the corners of my eyes, then bursting forth in shattering gusts, thick tears pour like blood from an open wound. I feel like Weeping Girl, a painting Risto has just completed, my feelings all inside out splintering in a million pieces. Is it my latest portrait?

I go to the couch blinded, tumbling Frère aside, and lie there in a wondering, turbulent state. If half of yourself is gone, does it mean you are worth only half of your former self?

It is hard to define
That line
Where dreams begin.

And end?

Risto does not know I am three months pregnant.

I am surprised it has not happened long ago.

1938 September Paris-Cannes

REALITY

19.

It is hard to define
The line
Where dreams begin.
Goodness and sin,
Sea and sky,
Have more distinction, it seems,
Than dreams.
Walk in the mists
Of Paris in January.
Frost in the air
Obscures all edges
Where dream and reality
Come together,
And a little of each rubs off.

My reality is Mireilles, born in January 1936, almost nine years to the day from my first meeting with Risto. From my dream – my world with him – emerges a little girl child, no longer an infant now, going on three years of age in the coming January, toddling and running, curious and loving, shining with life and flashes of sweetness.

Over three years have passed since the letter. I have not seen him since. Nor have I wished to. Pregnant, unhappy, initially, any desire for him was repressed. It was as if he had never existed.

I have been living these past years at my father's house on Avenue Victor Hugo with Maman. Olga has been caring for her in her widowhood, and now, with my baby and me, we are a world of women, except for Monsieur Héberd, and especially Pierre Bonnard with his extravagantly gentle letters and an occasional visit to see me at the house on Avenue Victor Hugo. He understands all. Even Suzelle forgives my indiscretions and rallies strongly. Pregnant with her first child, my baby, Miri, delights her. I count myself lucky to have friends of such fortitude to see me through the hazy thicket in which Risto left me. I am emerging from the brush and shrub that seemed to choke, and can finally see the open sky.

Maman says repeatedly that I am too thin and have shadowy circles under my eyes. "You must leave Paris. Go south. You should be away from all this talk of war, not that any one of us is prepared. Change will be good for you. I'll keep the child and Frère. A little visit will restore you."

Although my personal crisis seems large, the German Reich had annexed Austria last March, a remote event it seemed to me, but one causing consternation in Paris and all over Europe. Maman is right. I decide to return to the enchanting inn in Cannes for a visit to challenge myself and memory.

It is early September, and at L'Auberge du Citronnier many of the tourists are already gone. The proprietors, Monsieur and Madame de Brantes are glad to see me and give me the little room with the balcony overlooking the courtyard. Young Jacques, the owners' son, is about to be married to a local girl and there is much excitement at the inn.

My room is exactly the same with the large, white-cloaked bed, and fresh narcissus in a ceramic pot on the chest of drawers. Geraniums grow in tubs against the black iron balustrade on the balcony. The room looks as pure as the love I have felt here before, a love embraced by these four walls. I find, with relief, its re-embrace does not disturb me. I feel at peace. I plan to walk along La Croisette and swim to the wooden raft, lazing in the water like a skinny walrus. I will bask in the pale sun, surrounded by the aquamarine calmness of that most decorative of seas, the Mediterranean.

It is late afternoon. I am lying on the cover of the bed, shoes off, dress rumpled around me, in drifting contemplation of the past years, since my world of Risto had abruptly come to a halt. Life itself made it imperative to continue. I managed to survive through a healthy pregnancy and *accouchment*, *chez* Maman.

Maman has been a wonder! With open arms and eyes and heart, she took me to my old home, the house on Avenue Victor Hugo, barricaded the great front door with its brass knocker against strangers and sat the whole thing out with me. She gave me the strength to deliver and nurture yet another human being, her dark-eyed granddaughter, Mireilles, named, for Risto's sister, who had died at the age of 15 from tuberculosis. I did not tell Maman this. She would not have understood.

And, of course, Risto was gone from me – completely. He had no idea of the birth or that he had a tiny daughter, product of our love. I had determined he would never know. He did not deserve it.

Maman had informed Monsieur Héberd that I was taken ill, arranging for the doctor and the baby clothes and equipment, closeting me from prying eyes and curious questioners, when they discovered I was suddenly living at home. Since my father's death, she had had no large purpose, and I became her cause with never a reproach.

She told the world that I had been married, was now a Madame Ruy Aristide, a name I suggested, and although she looked at me from the corners of her eyes with disapproval, she accepted its inevitability. But the man – Risto – the father – was never mentioned.

It was only long after the birth of the baby, after I began to work part-time again for Monsieur Héberd, that I discovered Risto had been trying to contact me. There had been several letters.

"I cannot keep secrets," Maman had admitted. It was a summer night with the shades drawn in the salon and the lights dim to keep the room cool. Maman was sewing in the wing chair, mending a little dress of Miri's.

"What secrets, Maman?"

"The secrets of...well...the letters."

She put down her sewing and looked at me unblinking. "I feel better, having told you," she said.

"You've told me nothing! What letters?" I had started to tremble.

"The ones in the blue envelopes."

"They were from Risto!"

"I believe so."

"Why didn't you let me have them? How dare you intercept them! They were mine!"

"I was afraid they would hurt you...bring up the whole ugly business again. You were in no condition to be upset..."

"But they were my property. Why, it's against the law."

"I thought it best."

"Did you read them?"

"Don't be silly."

"What did you do with them?"

"Put them in the trash." She said this emphatically.

"How many have there been?"

"Perhaps a dozen or so...but not any in the last three months. None at all. That should tell you something."

"You must never intercept my letters again, Maman," I had blurted out, standing before her. "Promise me!" She had given an affirmative nod. Maman's unconditional love evidently had one limitation: to keep me from Risto at all costs.

He must have discovered my whereabouts through the concierge at 44, rue La Boëtie, a curious old woman, certainly not from Monsieur Héberd.

Just what had he wanted to say! "A total loss," I say out loud to the walls of my room at L'Auberge du Citronnier. "I'll never know!"

I rise from the white bed and, descend the single staircase to the ground floor of the inn. I enter the saffron-walled dining room with Norman-like beams in the ceiling. I find a table with a window on the court, overlooking the lemon tree, with a single carnation in a copper holder at the center. I order dinner from the winsome bride-to-be of Jacques de Brantes – a chervil *omelette*, salad and a *crème caramel*. It is a child's dinner, delicate in flavor. I order a *demi-bouteille* of white wine from Jacques behind the bar.

The young woman serves me neatly. Her name is Jeanne, and at the end of the repast, Madame de Brantes leaves her cloakroom.

"Did you enjoy the dinner?" she says approaching my table. Madame de Brantes, a plump woman in her mid-forties, beams with good will.

"Would you like a little of the chocolate-mousse cake? It's superb… or perhaps some fresh fruit? The peaches are exceptional."

"Oh, no. No, thank you," I reply.

"Maybe a liqueur? A cognac…Drambuie?" she purrs at me.

"No, really, thank you."

"Will Monsieur Risto be joining you?"

"No. No." I fumble with my string bag and rise to leave. "I hardly expect so."

Madame de Brantes colors with confusion.

"Excuse me…I only thought…he is here in the south. He dined here last week…staying at the Hôtel de La Ville in Mougins…not far you know. I just thought…"

I hasten to the bar to pay the check leaving her in mid-sentence. In my room, I sit panting on the bed, the bland supper churning in my stomach.

Should I pack up and leave? Risto usually has returned to Paris by September 1st and it is already the 6th.

But I do not leave. I decide not to be flushed out of my L'Auberge du Citronnier simply by Risto's presence in the area. It is unlikely we should meet and if we do, I will pass him by with a curt nod. Yet, what if he should dine again downstairs?

I will stay! I am to lunch with Monsieur Bonnard at Basso's tomorrow, something I have no intention of missing. No, Risto. You will not make me run.

I sleep fitfully and in the early morning go down past La Croisette and plunge into the Mediterranean. The swim I take is filled with memories of another summer, a wooden raft, and I can almost see elemental figures in stone standing in the hills that ring the sea. Later, I make my way to the terrace at Basso's and await my host. I have brought a notebook of my poetry to show Monsieur Bonnard, should the time be ripe to do so. Dressed in white linen, hair still damp from the sea, I sit there and watch the straggling crowd along the broad avenue until Monsieur Bonnard arrives with a flat package under his arm and a twinkling smile on his face.

"Ah, Camille...you look well...a little thin, perhaps...I do hope you're enjoying Cannes." He kisses me on the cheek, and I smell the faint aroma of sandalwood.

"I swam this morning. It's been a long time...and I love the water. Always have. My father taught me ...in Dinard in the summers."

We order guinea fowl, grilled over fennel leaves and a local *vin rosé*, after which he presents me with the flat package.

"I thought you might like this," he says shyly.

I eagerly unwrap the gift from its brown paper and find a painting of flowers in mauve and lavender and orange, held in a ceramic yellow pitcher.

"Oh," I burst out. "It takes my breath away. I'm thrilled. What a marvelous present! Monsieur Bonnard...I will treasure this...always." And, so saying, I leap up to kiss him again on the sandalwood cheek.

"You do like it? I though it looked like you...very feminine..."

Between the fragrant guinea fowl, the *vin rosé* and the flower painting propped on a chair opposite, time escapes too quickly.

"Next to seeing you, the best part of this special day is your present to me," I say laying down my fork and looking long at the floral picture.

"Then you do like it?"

"How could I not? It so lifts my spirits!"

"Do they need lifting?"

"Often," I reply with a laugh.

"Mine too," Monsieur Bonnard replies lighting a cheroot. "The trouble with me is I never seem to finish my painting. I always see something more to be done. Once I even touched up a picture when it was already hanging in a museum."

"You didn't!"

"Indeed I did. I sneaked in a tiny paint box and brush, and when the guards back was turned...*voila*. There was a brand new pink flower right where I wanted it. I wonder if the guard ever noticed."

We laugh, heads together, and I make him swear never to touch the painting he has given me because it is perfect.

Finally, over *café filtres,* I decide to present him with my booklet of poetry.

"I would love to have you read this...for your opinion...you may keep it if you like," I say, handing over to him 'Where Dreams Begin' in my spirally script.

"I'd be delighted. I didn't know you were writing poetry. It becomes you, you know. I have always loved books. Literature was my best subject at the Académie, not art. Would you mind if I read the title poem now?"

And he does so in a soft, sonorous voice.

At the end, he looks at me through steel-rimmed glasses and says, "Have you ever thought of publishing? This is exceptional and if the others are as good...?"

I tell him that Monsieur Héberd at the bookstore has suggested the same. Monsieur Bonnard takes down the address.

"I'll get in touch with him. We'll see what we can do. I really think it is worth exploring, don't you?"

"Well, of course it would be wonderful," I exclaim, and our meal almost ends on this happy note.

"Have you seen him?" he asks.

"No."

"Do you plan to? You know he's here...in Mougins."

"No."

"Does he know about the baby?"

"No."

"Camille, keeping it from him might be dangerous in the future – for him and for the child. Don't you think he has the right to know?"

"No."

"And Mireilles? Will you tell her when she is older who her father is?"

"No."

"It's her blood right too."

I have no comment, but my face is white enough to match my dress.

NO!

20.

THE QUESTION OF TELLING Risto of the fact of Mireilles and Mireilles eventually the truth of her heritage, I put from my mind in the next two days. Instead, I enjoy the golden weather, the lazy water, an occasional afternoon rain, in which I walk with delight, and simple feasts at night in the saffron dining room. My Bonnard flower painting is propped on the chest of drawers in my bedroom.

I plan to leave in the morning, and this evening I begin to pack my belongings in the old valise, but pause in my efforts to stand on the balcony and drink in the scented evening air. Suddenly, I see Risto rush through the court-yard below me beneath the lemon tree and into the front door of the inn.

I have no time to think. I hear the front door slam below, followed by swift footsteps on the stairs and in the hall. The door to my room – unlocked – is hurled open by a hand so merciless, it is almost ripped from its hinges.

Risto is before me in long shorts and a shirt. The presence I had not seen for so long is stunning in its intensity. He is like a criminal returning to the scene of a crime.

He shuts the door firmly behind him, leans back against it and remains immobile. As do I. The silence seems to vibrate between us.

"What a way to enter a room!" I finally say, in a voice as resolute as I can muster.

Risto goes to the straight chair next to the double glass doors leading to the balcony and sits down.

"How long do you expect to stay sitting on that chair?" I ask, unnerved by his boldness.

"As long as necessary."

"I don't know what that means."

"Aren't you interested in why I've come?" he says quickly.

"Not in the least." I try to stand as erect as I can. "Well, why are you here?"

"You have no idea?"

"No. I really can't imagine what brings you here in such violent fashion after all this time."

He rises and comes very close to me. "Have you already forgotten me?"

"That's ridiculous."

"You've been avoiding me. Why have you been running from me?"

"Who says I've been running?"

"It's obvious. You have been hiding from me for more than three years. I have written countless times but never an answering letter. I only heard of your presence here by sheer chance."

"And so?"

"Is that all you have to say?" Risto is pale and angry.

"You've certainly appeared quite rudely," I say, walking past him toward the balcony doors, open to a night filled with the fragrance of wisteria, removing myself from the closeness of his person. "How did you dare assume it would be convenient, may I ask? I might have had an engagement..." and I add with a tinge of maliciousness, "I might have been occupied."

"I almost expected as much," he breaks in, his tone consciously indifferent, but I have startled him for he glances suspiciously around the small pristine room. Then, drawn to the Bonnard painting on my bureau, he moves toward it to inspect it.

"When did you acquire this?"

"Monsieur Bonnard gave it to me just the other day."

"Why must you always call him Monsieur Bonnard? Why not Pierre?"

"Because I respect him so much."

"Perhaps you should call me Monsieur Risto!" He turns back to the bureau top, investigating my things laid out there – a small ring, some francs spread out on the wood – a box of powder. He touches each object and picking up a necklace I had bought for myself at a kiosk on La Croisette yesterday, he waves it at me. "And this?"

"What does it look like? It's a coral necklace."

"Well, obviously. I have two eyes. Who gave it to you?"

"No one you know," I say, playing the little game. He thinks I have a lover! "I don't know why it should interest you."

Risto throws the necklace back on the bureau top with a clank.

"I get compliments on it every time I wear it," I continue.

"That will do!" he says furiously.

I sit down on the edge of the bed with my back to him. He remains standing at the bureau, head down like a sullen boy. Surreptitiously I watch him in the looking glass.

"Cammy!"

I say nothing.

"Cammy." He turns and stands in front of me, then suddenly drops to his knees. Now my face is above his, the dominant one.

"I have looked for you everywhere," he begins softly. "It's been torture...the nights...you're in the candlelight...under a street light. Is that Cammy?" He says this simply. "Is there no way for us to be together again?"

I shake my head.

"Why? I've been frantic, missing you."

I give a soft laugh.

"You're laughing." He stands up abruptly. "You're making fun of me...you're...You do have a lover!"

"No. I have no lover."

"Ah…" escapes him. He seems to relax with this admission. He is bending over me.

It is my turn to stand before he lays a finger on me. "You must understand something," I say firmly. "Even a wife – which I obviously am not nor ever was – won't be found waiting patiently in the wings when you choose to come back. You are demanding and spoiled."

"Spoiled, yes…by you," he breaks in. "Spoiled for any other."

"It hasn't seemed to have stopped you. I'm not as stupid as I look, Risto. You are frantic because you're accustomed to getting exactly what you want!"

"Cammy…"

"You want to lead your own life?" I continue. "Well, go ahead! But for God's sake, let me lead mine in peace."

I am surprised to find tears in my eyes, for I had felt so sure. "I know you're still with that…Evangeline…It's mentioned all the time in the papers – with her flat bottom and her trousers and her bright red nails. Does she know you're here? Is she waiting for you in Mougins?"

"Now you sound like Rose!"

"How dare you approach me again?"

"I won't let you talk this way, Cammy."

"Don't tell me how to talk!" I'm astonished by my vehemence. So is Risto. "Ah, you don't like it when I criticize your way of living. That's it, isn't it? I am not allowed to judge you."

He walks toward me, pale with indignation. "I won't let you speak this way – ruin the Cammy I know."

The man is scolding me! "Won't let me? How dare you!"

"This is no way for you to speak…Nasty little pokes at me – at Evangeline…like the old ladies who sit in deck chairs along the boardwalk."

"Oh, Risto, don't be so pompous."

"There are certain things I expect of you – certain ways of behaving," he continues loftily. "Being unkind and so angry are not the ways you should behave. You have never been cruel."

"Oh, why did you seek me out? Why did you find me?"

"I had to. When I knew you were here, at the inn…I had to come." His shoulders lift in a kind of despair, but I detect cunning in the movement.

"How very pleased with yourself you must be!" he continues, suddenly on the attack. "Making me beg! I need you Cammy. I admit it. Even my work suffers. They call it cold, without heart."

"So, you come here, bursting in on me, because of your work?"

"Of course not. Have you heard nothing I've said? For a year after we parted, I didn't paint at all. I couldn't. Art was dead to me. You were not in my life. I didn't put brush to canvas. I blame you for that."

"Have you ever thought of blaming yourself, Risto? It was you who threw me away. You never considered what would be left for me… after you."

He does not answer directly, but instead, turns away from me and seems to ramble. "I used to wake at night, thinking I heard your voice. I'd walk by Héberd's after it closed thinking you might still be inside. Cammy…with her Breton hat with red ribbons…you, devouring your *petit pain au chocolat*. And as a woman, emerging from the sea, dripping with salt water like one of the Sirens."

His sincerity touches me. "Did you really think those things?"

"It's true."

"It…comes too late."

"Haven't you missed me?" There is a long pause. "Well, you will mourn me. You will grieve," Risto says, his face shutting down.

"I already have. Can't you see, I already am?"

"Don't reproach me …" he continues, anger in his eyes. "I never once spoke of the future. I loved you each minute, each hour as if we were both born the same day. I forgot I was born so many years before. There were no promises, Camille."

Speaking quickly, I say, "Go. Please go. It's too late."

Risto looks tired. He walks disjointedly to the door, slamming it shut as violently as he opened it, leaving only the sound of his footsteps on the stair.

I go to the balcony to see him emerge from the door of L'Auberge du Citronnier. He stops abruptly in the courtyard, beneath the lemon tree. He does not look up to my room, then hunches his shoulders and continues to the street, rue Mistral, outside the gate of the inn. His footsteps recede like bells in an empty church.

On the balcony I look up at the sky. There are no stars. I fill my lungs with fresh air.

I have my Miri. Risto still loves me. And I have been able to say No!

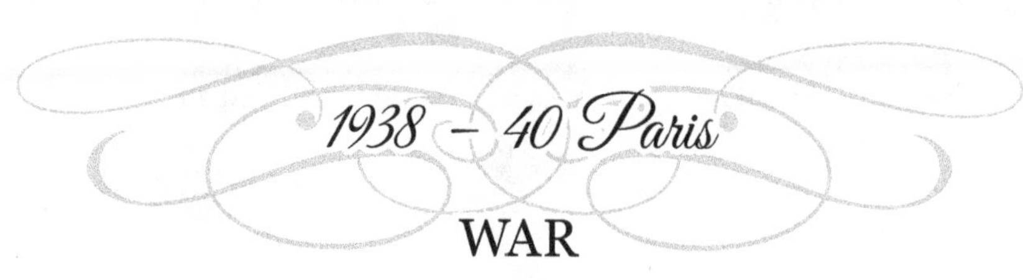

21.

LE *TRAIN BLEU* BACK to Paris, this September, 1938, is not "blue" for I return, eager to see my child, refreshed, and clutching my Bonnard painting. The train is not so crowded as it would have been "*en saison*," and the food in the luxury dining car is of the freshest.

My thoughts of Risto are tumultuous, including a sense of elation. Somewhere I have won, but I do not know the prize. Somewhere inside him I still exist in an intense way.

Within a matter of days, after arriving at Maman's on Avenue Victor Hugo, the first of many letters from him arrives. It is in the same blue envelope. I have taken to inspecting the mail in my bathrobe in the early morning, as in days of old, to avoid any destructive temptation in Maman.

It is a brief letter filled with injured pride, accusing me of being cold. Then, taking the coldness upon himself, he claims his work has turned to ice. He has the gall to accuse me of stealing from him his art!

Typical! He blames me for what his critics say, dramatizing the loss of his abilities when he is the most celebrated artist in Paris!

Risto is exhibiting all over, in gallery after gallery. No one dealer has exclusivity over his work. They all have tried. In England he is showing in London, in Liverpool and in Leeds. In America, his work appears at the Valentine Gallery in New York and 24 of his works are at the

Museum of Modern Art in Boston. There are countless pictures and sculptures in his native Spain, in Madrid and Barcelona.

For me, the fall of 1938 progresses with the bookshop, my mother, Frère, who is aging, and a continual stream of letters from Risto. Above all, I have my child. The two of us, with a slower Frère, walk every afternoon in the Bois after I am through with my duties at Héberd's. In the fragrant park, Miri meets her friends and plays among the musky leaves to the point she comes tripping back to me shoelaces undone, a scratch on the cheek, her hem torn and hanging. I appraise the degree of harm and only have to look at the shimmering face with the dark eyes, to know that all is well. I am not the daughter of an insurance assessor for nothing!

On our journey home we buy sizzling chestnuts. We return to the sharp cider and buttered bread on Maman's round coffee table in the salon at Avenue Victor Hugo with her best Limoges plates set out for the three of us.

Frequent letters from Risto continue. I finally respond rather formally at first. He keeps me posted on his art progress, and I write as encouraging letters as I can. I really do not want him to think me 'cold'. There is no talk of love until one day in late November, the *poste* arrives with a larger envelope than usual, but in the same blue color. Inside I find a drawing of me, nude, voluptuously lying on a wooden raft in the middle of the sea. The figure is not abstract as all. The lines of the body undulate. Now, that is love talk!

The letters are there for me through the winter and into spring. They acquire a certain urgency. He must see me! I dismiss these requests from my mind, and I do not meet with Risto.

Since my trip to Cannes in the early fall, and my confrontation with him, I find it much easier for me to work at Héberd's on the street where he lives and near his studio.

Before the trip it had caused me pain to know he was so close. I was in terror of seeing him. But this winter of 1938-39 passes with lesser ache. One spring day, Risto comes to the shop in search of me when I am out for lunch. Monsieur Héberd chases him from the store, brandishing a heavy dictionary.

In May, I see for the first time the name 'Artistide', no *nom de plume*, in print in the Paris Review! Pierre Bonnard had written a letter to Monsieur Héberd during the past fall as promised, suggesting I submit a piece, with Héberd's help, to the small literary monthly that specializes in aspiring writers. I had embraced the idea and had sent in two poems, "Where Dreams Begin' and 'Cock's Crow', 'Where Dreams Begin' was accepted. 'Cock's Crow' was kept for possible future publication. The poems were submitted under the single name 'Aristide'. Risto's use of a single name had inspired me to do the same.

As summer comes, the fatal summer of 1939, my elation is diminished. There is constant talk of war. Some believe it will happen. There are those who spoil for a fight. Mostly, people feel safe behind the Maginot Line. The markets of Paris are still full, so rich we walk through Les Halles only to enjoy the smell of fresh produce, neat bundles of parsley and new shallots, bay leaves and fat green-and-white leeks.

The fight in Europe begins in earnest in September, 1939, when the Germans invade Poland. And before the Germans come to Paris in booted droves, before it is over for France, even while still digging trenches in the soft earth of the Bois, we talk of the 'phony war', 'the war in disguise', like so many jungle beasts without the sense of sight, blind to reality, blind to the laws of war, our drive for survival missing. The one who truly worries is Maman. She worries for me, for Miri.

I worry for Risto. He writes of his anxieties.

> "Hitler has personally placed my works on the decadent list. You'd think he wouldn't have time to worry about such things. Do you suppose the Germans will destroy my canvases if they get here? At least the Americans like me! There is to be a retrospective at the Museum of Modern Art running through next January and then to tour the United States. I shipped a few pieces. I hope they survive the U-boats.

> For the rest, I am frantically trying to hide my works. Also my collection of other artists. Some of them are vastly valuable, and not being 'decadent' the Germans might rob me of them. They do that sort of thing. Do you suppose they'd melt down my metal pieces for guns? The bastards! I have been moving these by hand cart across Paris to a special silo outside the city. I am moving to Royan, bag and baggage, canvas and paint. And you, my little girl? By all means, get out of Paris."

This panicky letter chills me. Where is Rose? Where is Roberto? Evangeline?

Risto's departure for Royan on France's Atlantic coast north of Bordeaux seems more final in its bereavement than the war itself. Physical distance between us, from city to city, county to country, has always caused me irrational pain.

However, his letters continue from Royan with an occasional snapshot of him – in his studio, in a straw hat, seated in the grass over a picnic lunch, never snapshots with other people. Or there will be a little drawing of a woman's face (mine) or a small Harlequin.

One day, after three weeks of silence, there is only a postcard, instead of the blue envelope, and I know he has fallen in love again. This depresses me more than my own departure from Paris. Maman is insisting Mireilles and I go to the south of France.

"I'm not leaving you here alone," I tell her. "You must come with us. You've been so good to us. I won't leave without you!"

She is adamant. Her place is in Paris. She has volunteered at L'Hôpital Saint-Just. It has hardly reached the point of being full of the wounded, but soon that will change. Soon, it will be crammed with mutilated young men, jammed into the halls and corridors and down in the basement with the pipes.

"You have a little child to protect, Camille," Maman says. "That must come first. And you're a young woman. I want you out of Paris before a foreign soldier sets foot in it. This house, the house of your father, this city, has been my whole world. He would want me to remain where I belong."

It is with reluctant movements I prepare to leave Maman. I write Pierre Bonnard, that most sterling of friends, and ask him if he knows of a possible safe haven.

He replies within three weeks describing a little town called Vence, near Grasse, not too far from Cannes. 'I will expect you for frequent lunches at Basso's to forget this hideous conflict. Vence would be the safest place off the coast itself and out of range should there be direct fire from the sea.' He had gone so far as to put down a sum of money to hold a small stone house there for my arrival. 'Just let me know when'.

Leaving a forwarding address at the *poste*, packing my wooden chest with its brass fittings, full of letters, photographs, drawings, my poetry notebooks, stashing clothes and children's books in several string bags, I take leave of Maman. We cling to one another in desperation. Will I ever see her again? My dear Maman. Will she ever see Mireilles grown? Will any of us survive?

Miri and I take *Le Train Bleu* on an evening in March, 1940, a far different kind of trip than any I have experienced. It is filled with people leaving Paris, and it is still early in the game of war. At a later date, as the Germans are about to enter Paris in mid-June, the train will become as tightly packed as the leaves in a book. Petain will sign an armistice with the Germans, and for all who have not left Paris, it will be too late. The city will close down.

On *Le Train Bleu,* I travel like a gypsy with baggage, an older Frère in a despised box, Miri's clutched hand obsessively in my own.

The dining car has been commandeered so we eat in our seats on fruit and bread Maman has had the foresight to supply. Fortunately, Frère like grapes. Maman will send more belongings once I am settled – Bonnard's painting, Papa's Aubusson rug, left to her in his will which she has given to me, and some household equipment.

She has also provided me with a small allowance from the trust body of Papa's estate. I plan to get employment, but who knows what work I will find in the little town of Vence.

Miri and I are off on an adventure with a huge question mark at its end. Risto is in Royan, I think of the three of us, plus Maman, as scattered from one end of France to the other. It is a strange 'family' because the man does not know he has fathered a child nor has the child ever heard nor seen her natural sire.

None of that matters.

It is enough that I alone know the truth.

SHADOWS

22.

MIRI AND I ARE living in the small stone house Monsieur Bonnard has found for us in the town of Vence in the Alpes-Maritimes north of Cannes. It is the summer of 1943. With its cobbled streets and one of two three-star restaurants, our village normally attracts any number of travelers. They have usually come into our hills to the town, which smells deliciously of garlic and of the fruity Mediterranean olive oil, particularly at supper time. Or so I am told. But, being wartime, few strangers pass our way.

Vence is near the town of Grasse, "The Perfume Capital of the World," where the best 'noses' select elixirs to be sent to the great perfume houses in Paris. These experts pick out the scents from enormous fields of flowers that grow throughout Grasse. The fragrance of Grasse is noticeable kilometers away, as Miri and I discover on a picnic near there, earlier this spring, our own tomatoes, fresh cheese, black olives *Niçoise,* and bread drizzled with olive oil, spread out before us.

The war does not seem to affect the perfume business. It is thriving, the perfumes sent to the Reichstag to enhance the allure of Nazi ladies.

Our house, too, has a garden, forming an enclosed citadel, with eggplant and tomatoes and peppers, red and green. These, too, are fragrant. I am busy on summer evenings making marmalades and vegetable sauces with wax tops to be used in winter.

I work in the library of the local school, L'École des Palmiers, and certain hours in the office of the Directeur. The building itself is forbidding, and bleak in winter, but my working there will permit my daughter to receive her education free.

Miri is seven, unusual looking rather than beautiful, much the way I was at her age. Although the eyes are as brown-black as any senorita's, she has blonde hair, a curving cheek line like my own, and a nose a bit too large for her face.

We have been here just over three years. For me, it has not been a bad life, centered around my daughter who turns a burnished tan in summer beneath the frothy yellow mimosa trees, color inherited from the father of whom she knows nothing. She believes a man named Ruy Aristide, sired her, and died shortly after her birth. She has accepted this unquestioningly. For the townspeople of Vence, I am merely Madame Ruy Aristide, the youngish widow with a little girl to raise.

I ache for Maman. I ache for Paris, for Risto too. Communication is spotty. Sometimes I will receive a large packet of letters and then weeks will pass without a word. When the paper bundle arrives, I unfold the crisp pages and read between the lines.

Risto is flushed out by the Germans in Royan. He returns to Paris. He has a new studio with a marvelous stove but no fuel. As he sleeps there, he is outrageously cold. He writes to me that he refuses special favors from the Germans, but he did give a souvenir photograph of the huge painting War, depicting devastation on a monumental scale, to a Nazi officer who asked him, "Did you do this?" to which Risto replied, "No, you did!" He is proud of his remark.

In one letter, he is in turmoil because French soldiers in Gisors damage some sculptural pieces at Château de Chevauchers. The Germans have placed prisoners of war in his commandeered home. "I am not even allowed to go there!"

The letters from Maman, from the house of my father on Avenue Victor Hugo, are more domestic. Yet, she writes of hospital scenes of reversed tonality.

> "I have to treat the wounded. They are mostly Germans! It's very hard. They are so young! My house shakes and echoes like an empty pickle barrel when the allied bombers fly over it to their German targets. I open all the doors because of the pressure and the windows, too, so the panes won't shatter."

Her letters prompt me to volunteer two afternoons a week at the local Veterans Hospital where Allied wounded are sent to recuperate.

Maman is hungry. One letter arrives to describe a wondrous, new weekly pattern. One of her released French patients brings her fresh eggs on a regular basis.

> "He has a chicken coop in his back garden, and sometimes even chicken livers, and I am in for a feast! I save even the potato peelings for soup! You have no idea what one onion costs in Paris! And the greengrocer expects only cash if you are lucky enough to find one with an onion to his name. The fishmonger's boy – you remember him? Henri? Rather a loutish youngster, but I've changed my opinion because he comes, ringing his bell on his bicycle, when fish is suddenly available."

I write in return, never knowing whether my letters will be received. I write sitting at the window in the kitchen watching Miri among the herbs in the garden where she tends a patch of her own, Frère at my feet dreaming of spring.

I do not only write letters, I write poetry; poems about a war with which I feel I am shadowboxing; poems with titles like 'The Soldier', 'To Arms', and one, 'War', which suggests the agony in Risto's painting of the same name.

> Wails from children,
> Keens from women,
> Shrieks from birds,

Moans from flowers,
Cries from wood,
Sobs from stone,
Screams from furniture,
From beds, from chairs,
From curtains, pots, cats,
Papers, odors.

I do not submit these war poems to the Paris Review magazine. I do not even know if it is in operation or if my poetry will be received. I put the poems in the wooden chest with the letters from Risto and Maman and from Monsieur Bonnard who is in mourning for his precious Marthe. She succumbed last year to a cancerous disease. I write him often to raise his spirits as best I can, chattering on about Miri, our life, small adventures, poetry.

I even try to define the word DREAM, as not a person nor an idea of beauty, but as a vision. He loves this particular letter likening Marthe to a vision from his youth.

We arrange to meet. He has been reclusive, his eyesight, never good, is failing further, but we agree to lunch at Basso's among the mussels and lemons and sea breezes.

I persuade him to come home with me for supper, after which we sit at a garden table under the wisteria. It is early autumn and we drink coffee and eat grapes, the decanter of cognac near at hand. Only the crickets are heard except for an occasional far away shot in the hills from the direction of Grasse, the only dissonance.

Finally he mentions Marthe.

"Since she is gone...Do you know we were together 48 years? These have been lonely months."

"I'm sure." I touch his hand.

Turning to me, he continues, "I don't know how to say this...I've always been so fond of you...Will you let me...court you?"

I'm astounded. Finally I manage, "I don't know what to say," which he interrupts, "We've had our grand passions, you and I."

"Please, Monsieur Bonnard."

"Always 'Monsieur'? Still?" Then, "Am I too old?"

"Pierre...my 'grand passion'...he's your age. My feelings for him... they're still there."

We sit listening to the crickets. Truly, I believe he is relieved.

By the time Risto's letters arrive weeks may have passed. He is back in Paris. I find the words lifeless, his words cold. But, sometimes there is a picture – the minotaur with a girl that looks like me, or a passionate nude among flowers.

Sometimes, there is money. I accept it gratefully. More often, I receive his mood, either black with the occupation; "The Jews (Evangeline? Is she still with him?) ride around on bicycles, forced to wear yellow stars on their shirts!" He had written of his desire for the past, "the way we used to be."

What is the good of 'little black words' when my sensuous friend only comprehends passion? Yet when the blue envelope appears, I sit down for my moment alone with him, then lock the words away in the wooden chest under my bed.

Rose has died, he writes. She is just another shadow, like Marthe. Although Rose had long been gone from him, Risto now is truly free, and financially whole, always so important to him. I can tell when there is a new woman in his life, the moment the postcards arrive in lieu of letters. One would think, as he grew older, his lust for women would diminish, but it does not.

In response to a postcard in which he names Fabienne Bourreau "whom I occasionally use as model," I wrote back in anger. My resentment of the young woman made me want to join the hapless Rose and Marthe and my father. And his reply? "But then you wouldn't remember me, and I want to be remembered." How he would have wanted Mireilles to remember him, Miri, his finest creation! When Risto's current liaison seems to lose fire, the letters to me resume again, arriving in clumps like bouquets of flowers.

Risto still has no knowledge of the little girl he sired. She is mine alone, named for the dead sister of which he was so fond, inheriting his darker pigment of skin and the chocolate eyes, that is her legacy, not his name nor his acknowledgement nor his love.

I remember Risto's painting, Life, done before I was born. It showed a woman with a baby in arms facing a nude couple, the man embracing the younger woman with finger raised in protesting gesture to the mother of his child.

This is Risto's view of 'life', painted in cool, dispassionate blues. When his woman has a baby, Risto must look elsewhere. The mother and child become 'they' or 'them' as he used to refer to Rose and Roberto. With my silence, Miri and I will never be 'they' or 'them' to him.

Miri and I dine on skinny chicken stuffed with chestnuts for our dinner on Christmas Eve instead of the traditional lamb. I notice Frère sleeps through our meal. He does not beg in his usual way for a bit of crisp chicken skin. On Christmas Day, he does not rise to his feet at all. I find him lying before the grate in the salon. Slowly I sink beside him and cover his small, cold body with my own. He is gone, another shadow to haunt my dreams.

By mid-August, 1944. The Allies have moved toward Paris. Maman's letters change.

> "The street fighting between the French Resistance and the retreating Germans is horrible. The Hotel Crillon was badly shot up, and I barely dare go to the hospital or shopping for food, a terrible chore, the queues are so long."

Finally I receive the radiant letter from her written August 25th:

> "Every bell in the city is ringing. I didn't know there were still so many flowers. Where do they come from with all the trampling and trucks and bombs? But they are there on the American tanks that roll through the boulevards. Everyone is in tears. Everyone is kissing. Paris is ours again!"

Risto's words are more practical:

> "Maybe now I can get some decent pipe tobacco. The American machinery certainly makes a racket...but really it's a kind of music!"

Enclosed is a photograph of a bizarre sculpture, an American tank made of bits of scrap metal attached to a percolator lying on its side. Not so practical after all!

He is going to show in October at the *Salon d'Autonne* for the first time.

"They are calling this one *Salon de la Libération*. I have 74 paintings and several sculptures of which I am extremely proud since I did them all during the enemy occupation. The *Salon* committee is setting aside a special gallery for me. By the way, I have joined the Communist Party."

The Communist Party! He who so loves money! Even though he lives simply enough, in unmodish clothes and surroundings, Risto wants only top quality, be it a peasant dish of beans or a rough red wine. He also loves caviar and *Veuve Cliquot* and uses only the finest pigments. Besides, he has never been political in the least.

But a political creature he becomes when, as the *Salon de La Libération* opens, nasty demonstrations against his politics erupt in the special gallery itself and on the streets.

When I question why he joined the Communist Party, Risto replies:

"It's the logical conclusion of my life. I have always been an exile. The French Communist Party opened its arms to me, and I am among my brothers."

These events all take place away from me during this year of shadows, of passing and death and change and final joy. Our country belongs to its people once more.

Always, there is Mireilles. It is she alone who roots me to earth, to this Vence, to my beloved France.

1947 Summer Vence

THIRST

23.

RISTO WRITES ME FROM the Hôtel de la Ville in Mougins in early July, begging me to see him "for I cannot even love any more," although this has not stopped him from continuing to live in Paris with Fabienne.

I do not respond to his letter. When Monsieur Bonnard had died last year – yes, my dear friend is gone – I had attended the tiny service in Le Gannet on a bleak January day and had seen, from the rear of the church, Risto and Fabienne in the front pew. I had left before their heads had a chance to turn.

Another letter comes in August. It is from Cap d'Antibes to my little house in Vence, not a long distance at all. He asks to see me once again. His eloquence touches me when he says;

"We owe it to ourselves – we, who have somehow managed to survive the terrible war and have come out the other side. Meet me, if only to reaffirm life, to say to each other – we meant something!"

To reaffirm life! "Give me back my talent if only for one last grand painting." Accompanying the letter is a small pot of caviar.

Suddenly, I decide to meet with him at L'Auberge du Citronnier. I am not sure why. Curiosity perhaps? Or perhaps the letdown from the war will be lifted. Perhaps the empty space left by Monsieur Bonnard will be filled, but most probably because I was 38 years old last month and life is escaping me.

Vence had not offered much choice in male companionship. In my world, there had only been one young soldier sent to rehabilitate from wounds received in the North African campaign. I took care of him at the Hôpital des Invalides. He loved me enough to want me for his wife, but he was much younger than I, not only in years. He was just not enough...after Risto.

So, I tell Miri, I am meeting a friend for the weekend. She is incurious. Miri, now a tomboy, 11 years of age, can stay with a school friend and her parents. She is delighted with the arrangement..."the first time of many, Maman...I hope, I hope."

I find myself rushing through Cannes on a soft, August evening from the bus terminal. From the corner of rue Mistral, I see a figure standing under the street light in front of L'Auberge du Citronnier. It is Risto. He looks transfigured in the light coming from above him, shining on his body. His face is brown, the gleaming eyes golden. I approach slowly. He takes my hand without a word.

We walk through the courtyard, our footsteps echoing, and ascend to the room with the balcony overlooking the lemon tree we had shared more than once previous to the hideous war, previous to our own separation.

Nothing has changed. It is as if we had never been apart. I pass two days in a haze of renewed sensual memory. We barely leave the room, only to dine once downstairs served by the young wife of Jacques de Brantes. We feast on green vegetables from the kitchen garden at the inn and devour the fresh fish from the Mediterranean, and the red wine so pleasing to Risto's palate, then ascend to our sensual sanctuary.

"Come live with me again," Risto says softly, as we lie among the tangled white sheets.

"I cannot," I respond, visualizing in a flash my Miri. I rise from the bed, wrap a robe about my body and move to the balcony. Risto follows me, towel about his waist.

"Then, marry me, Cammy. Marry me – now. It's time. I have never been able to get over you. I suffer without you. I need the inspiration only you gave me so consistently. I want to marry you."

"What?" I say.

"Marry me. I don't know why I haven't thought of this before!"

"Neither do I."

"Please."

"It's impossible," I reply in a low voice. For a moment, it is as if I am looking into Miri's shadowed eyes, with their long lashes and secrets inside.

"Why? What's to stop us?" Risto persists. "It's not too late. You might even have a child. You'd like that, wouldn't you? Our child? What a great mother you'd be!"

Risto comes close to me at the railing. He takes both of my hands in his.

"My answer is NO." I pull away from him.

"I know you still love me. Haven't you proved it?"

"Love is never enough."

I go from the balcony into the bedroom and sit on the bed. He follows me. Settling beside me on the white spread, he again takes my hands.

"Why?" he asks.

I look down at the four hands in my lap, his brown and large, with flat fingers, mine, lighter in color. They are intertwined.

"It's too late!" I say.

"It's never too late for love."

"I'd become your victim, if I married you. You have many bodies strewn along the way."

"What rubbish!" he says, angry.

"I will not marry you. Thanks for asking but I will not."

"*Dieu*! I don't understand women – particularly you!"

"You were never able to answer for my future. Why should you now, at this point in our lives?"

"True," he says, humble. "But I'm able to now, really for the first time."

"Too bad it comes so late, this conscience, if you want to call it that. I have no future for you to worry about."

"You're being cruel, Cammy. I used to believe there was no meanness in you. I guess I was wrong."

Risto moves away from the bed and out onto the balcony again. He is sulking.

After a moment, I follow him and sit tentatively in one of the chairs.

"Risto, you know if we were to marry, in a matter of days or weeks, there'd be a beauty, an Evangeline or a Jacqueline or a Fabienne. It's your nature. Sometimes, I wish you had been an ordinary man."

"I don't want a raving beauty for a wife! I don't want a damned egoist out to grab everything she can get! I want safety and peace and quiet inspiration."

"I don't call our recent lovemaking safe and peaceful!"

"You're right there!" He laughs.

I stand beside him at the balcony railing overlooking the courtyard and the lemon tree.

"But I am an ordinary woman. And you came at me – never letting me up to breathe. You were always there. There are wives and there are lovers. Rarely do they come in one package!"

Risto lowers his eyes. It seems a door has shut.

"I could never be your wife," I continue. "I only accepted the other lady lovers all these years because I knew I had no right to you. At least there was a distance between us. If I were to marry you, there'd be no space. It would be too painful."

"And what if I foreswore all others?"

I give a little laugh.

"Now you laugh at me."

"Ah, no, no. I could never laugh at you."

"Cammy, try to understand. You have been describing the human condition. I'm only an apelike animal but one with a dream. We shared that dream – you as model - me as artist. We shared each other, breathed each other, at dawn, in beds, on rafts, and while the sun went down."

"You shared yourself very well indeed," I say wryly.

Moments pass.

"Cammy," he says. "Why have you come here? Why did you respond – in your letters, finally – here in this rendezvous?"

"Perhaps you are irresistible to me, Monsieur Risto – as in irresISTible," I say with a smile. "Maybe I feel immortalized by your paintings of me. Or maybe it's that once you told me 'No, Cammy. I must be free. You will never be able to go where I go, see what I see!' Maybe I wanted to prove you wrong." I look at him. "My answer to marriage is NO."

"You are making a tragedy of us."

"When you sent me away what did you think there was left for me?"

"You were young and loveable. The world awaited you."

"Remember, Risto, you sent me away. Then, there was the War. I said to myself, 'There was Risto. Risto, the War…' The two have driven me outside the times I live in."

Except for Mireilles, I say to myself. She has grounded me. And poetry has permitted me to soar.

"All these years, I have given you nothing," he is saying.

"That's not quite true. I have many beautiful pictures, some very valuable."

"Oh, them," he says, tossing his art away in a most astonishing way.

"You have given me more than you know."

Does he deserve to know Miri exists? Or would she become just another of his victims? With Risto I had been whole once. When he threw me away I was half. My daughter gave me back that lost half and I felt complete again. By telling him of her, would I again be back to a bereft fifty per-cent of my former self? Is the risk for Miri, or is the risk for me?

We sit side by side in chairs on the balcony looking out into the night. It is a limpid evening. Enough has been said.

Finally I ask, "How did you manage to send the pot of caviar! It's rare and hard to get."

"I have a friend who has Balkan connections and manages to get it for me."

"Evangeline? After all, she's part Yugoslav. Don't tell me you're still with her too!"

It is a most unfortunate moment.

"Of course not," he replies angrily, almost spitting the words. "I have many Yugoslav friends. Do you think me so unpopular? This is a male friend. You, who are so greedy for the little gray pearls, should be grateful."

"A male friend, indeed."

"His name is Théo. He was in the resistance in Yugoslavia – fled the Russians in 1944…"

"I thought you were a Communist. I thought you loved the Russians," I interject.

Ignoring my remarks, he says, "Théo is penniless – I let him tutor little Jean-Michel."

"And who is little Jean-Michel?"

Risto pauses a moment. "He is my son."

"Your son?" Communism is forgotten. "You mean Roberto?"

"Roberto is twenty-three," he says laughing.

"Jean-Michel?"

"Yes. Jean-Michel."

"And how old is…is…Jean-Michel?"

"He will be four soon."

"Who is the mother?" I say, still staring out into the night.

"He is Fabienne's."

Then, furiously, I rise to my feet and blurt, "Then, for God's sake, why don't you marry her?"

I hastily pack for the late bus. Risto still sits on the balcony chair, morose and deflated. He does not look up as I leave the room with my valise, yet I can feel his eyes boring into my back as I make my way with stumbling steps through the courtyard and into rue Mistral.

He will never know of Mireilles! She is more mine than ever she has been, a child of whom he will always be deprived!

Risto sprinkles children upon the earth like so many mustard seeds!

Part Three

1953 July Vence

MIRI'S DREAM

24.

So many years. I wrestle with memories: the pink linen clad bistro on an alley on a side street in Paris – Le Petit Clos; L'Auberge du Citronnier, in the cool breeze off the sea in Cannes. Above all, I remember the cold, misty avenue in Paris, before the window of Galeries Lafayette, and the moment when a stranger approached me through the *brume* and said, "Mademoiselle, you have an interesting face. I would like to make your portrait. I am Risto."

I have somehow, built the fabric of a life, weaving a cocoon in which Miri and I can dwell. She is a lively creature, now a young woman of 17. She has her moods, occasionally deep and black, as shadowed as her eyes, moods which I term her 'Spanish melancholy'. Perhaps her innocence protects her, although innocence has its price.

I have thus far been able to stave off and satisfactorily answer her questions, a father named Ruy Aristide, dying young. "What was he like, Maman?" "Handsome, with your dark eyes," I reply.

Our world, first, was comprised of a home with her grandmother, in the form of a sitting room-bedroom apartment in the great house near the Bois de Boulogne in Paris, then, the departure from the capital as the Germans were about to march in, and finally, a place in this tranquil world, this Vence.

She needs to know no more. I feel the truth of Risto would make her distrust her mother! Rightly so, for have I not set up a network of lies and omissions?

Miri's heritage appears, not only in her Spanish moods, but in an ability to draw. She is talented, not spectacularly so, but she does possess a gift, one that gives her joy. She is taking lessons in drawing from a lady in Cannes twice a week during the summer recess, taking the bus in early morning and returning at dusk. She always brings a gift – a bunch of primroses wrapped in white paper – or a parcel of fresh caught sardines she has purchased at the waterfront market in Cannes, to be grilled for supper.

It is a good life. Nearby Grasse, 'The Valley of Flowers', attracts tourists. They come to Vence as well for the Matisse chapel with its crucifix and magnificent stained glass windows, done by the ailing artist, so sick he had not lived out the year. He had been our most famed resident, a great friend of Bonnard. Sometime, in summer, the motor cars are bothersome, trying to maneuver the narrow, cobblestone streets, forcing us on foot to press against the buildings. It is a seasonal affliction. By late September, the quiet rhythm of life returns.

This is a lovely July day. Miri has departed for Cannes on the early bus. I receive an exciting pair of letters by *poste*, one from the magazine publisher who first presented my poetry, 'Where Dreams Begin', in 1949, now telling me they want to publish 'Cock's Crow'.

The other is a long letter from Risto. It arrives in its blue envelope and it is with a sense of luxury I open it, with time stretching ahead of me in which to savor it. The letter is from Vallauris. So near!

"My darling little girl; I am here in Vallauris to attend the bullfights. Cocteau is with me… and several more…it's quite a party."

> "Is there no way we can meet? You are so near and I am lonely for you. I am not so young, but my vigor remains, thank God. It is for you if you want it. It is love I feel for you. You are always there. You will never go away.
>
> Risto"

> "If I had never let you go when I saw you again that weekend after the war – if you had accepted a marriage then, think of all the hundreds and hundreds of days and nights – six years worth – for the reaping of love!
>
> R."

I decide to walk up the hill back of the street where I live. It is approached by a yellow path through the cypress trees and white alders.

As I make my way up the dirt road, pushing through the thick shadows of laurel bushes along the way, a heavy cloud passes above me, blocking the sun, letting single drops fall.

As I reach the top of the hill, it starts raining in earnest, a drenching summer rain, and I run back down the curling path to the dryness of my house, cool because of its stone walls, to write my letter to Risto.

I tell him there is no point in meeting. Since our parting so long ago, our infrequent trysts have not been worth the price, agonizing in the recovery from them, leaving me lost.

Yet, in truth, I see him in Mireilles every day, my Miri, the child he will never know. Let him have the others. Signing it "Cammy", I run to the *poste* through the lessening rain to mail it to Risto's Vallauris address. The drops come in spurts and gusts as I arrive home.

It is getting late. I must think about supper. Will Miri bring us some fish – maybe sea urchins so prevalent in the Mediterranean this season of the year? If not, I have a cutlet of veal in the cold chest – and some salad greens. She is late. Her bus must have been delayed by the rain. Sometimes the road is partially washed out.

Even as I think this, I hear the front door bang and her running steps. She comes into the kitchen, wet and glowing. Children are freshened by the rain like flowers. Their faces gleam with innocence.

But what I see before me is not a child reborn in the rain. Mireilles is a young woman close to 18. Her look is stunning. Her wettened dress outlines a lush body so like my own. She stands taller than I do, legs long perhaps from walking the Vence hills, and the smoky eyes glisten like her father's.

She carries her sketchpad in an oilskin wrapper, a box of colored pencils, a package from the confectioner's shop she frequents in Cannes, and her string bag. She also brings pink flowers wrapped in paper.

She flashes the package to me, with an exuberant "Pralines, Maman. You know how you love them!" She is just as addicted. She throws down her belongings on the table and opening the ice chest asks. "What's for supper?"

"I guess the cutlet," I reply. "Did the class go well? I want to see your drawings. And you better take off those wet clothes," I say, placing the blooms in a glass pitcher.

"In a minute. In a minute." Miri is busily peeling an orange, engrossed in pulling away the white pulp form the fruit.

"Out of that wet dress, please, young lady."

"Oh, Maman," she says crossly. "Don't you want to hear my adventure?"

"Stop teasing. Of course I want to hear your adventure, but first I want you dry." Her wet clothes are beginning to form a puddle on the floor. "You look as if you're melting."

"Guess what?" She slides out of her cotton dress, which forms a damp, blue bundle on the floor, and stands before me in her chemise. Her rounded body is smooth and so womanly, I look at her almost shyly.

"What? Must I guess?"

"Yes." I turn to the sink with its basket of lettuce and begin pulling apart the leaves.

"All right. You bought a new dress."

"Wrong."

"You found a puppy you want to keep?"

"No!"

"You did a marvelous drawing and all the instructors gathered around and wanted to give you a prize."

"I only wish."

"I give up."

"I met a man today."

I look up from the lettuce with unease.

"Where? At sketch class?"

"No, no, on the street...in front of the confectioner's window. He just came up to me."

"On the street?"

"Yes. He was suddenly there. It had just started to rain."

"A man? What...?"

"He was not a young man...although his face was young. His hair was white, and he was brown from the sun."

"He just came up to you like that? You know what I've warned you about. Really, Miri."

"But it wasn't like that, Maman. He was very polite...oh, maybe a bit intense, actually. He kind of studied me, and when I told him my mane was Mireilles, he looked so strange. He said he had a sister once named Mireilles who died as a girl. Then he asked to paint a portrait of me! Can you imagine? Me to be painted? I told him I must ask your permission, and he said he would be back in front of the confectioner's shop on Thursday – I have my next sketch lesson then, you know – at the exact same time for my answer. Oh, may I Maman? To be painted! What a dream, Maman. Oh, may I be painted? Please?"

She is chattering, but I have long since stopped listening and feel as if, like Miri's blue dress, I had melted into a puddle on the tile floor of my kitchen in a stone house in the town of Vence in the Alpes-Maritimes north of Cannes near Grasse.

"Stop dreaming, Mireilles! It's absolutely the wrong dream!" I say this so harshly, she drops the orange and runs upstairs, as I stand shaking and in shock. Risto! Risto is near and for the first time, I am mortally afraid.

PHOENIX

25.

MY DAUGHTER PESTERS ME all evening over the cutlet, over the dishes, over the sketchpad in the salon with its grate now filled with summer flowers.

"Why won't you answer, Maman. It would be exciting to sit for an artist! Oh, please, Maman. At least, think about it."

I cannot think at all, and pleading headache and ill temper, I say I am tired.

"You do look awfully pale, Maman." I go up the stairs to my bedroom. I sit on the edge of the bed for a long time. Finally I hear Miri rustling around in the room next to me, preparing for sleep. I hear her switch off the light.

I sit there, unmoving, well into the night. Finally, I move quietly to retrieve from beneath my bed the wooden chest with brass corners and lock and key in which my blue envelopes are kept.

Opening it, I see the familiar letters. There are hundreds of them. I have never counted. The last, received this very morning is on top, with its Vallauris postmark.

There must have been no bullfight this afternoon. It is Monday and so many things close. Risto must have gone to Cannes to amuse himself for the afternoon, and he found Miri.

Today – the meeting in Cannes – demands action. With revulsion, I shiver. Did he see something of me in our daughter's face? Or was it merely the licentiousness of an old goat approaching a delicious young girl?

I could never have envisioned this. I have created such a terrible trap for my daughter and for myself? How can I tell her? Where are the words?

I panic. Risto has doomed me to become a vagabond again. I will run as I had from 44, rue la Boëtie that day in June 1935, when I had gone home to Avenue Victor Hugo to have my baby and hide. I will take Miri and leave our gentle life, cutting my losses, closing the stone house. I decide this while kneeling on the floor before my chest as if praying there. One thing is certain. The letters must be destroyed, snapping at last, the thread that draws me toward that time, that place, toward love, toward him.

First, I read the letters into the night – every one. Time is devoured by the avariciousness of that love, developing on paper in front of my eyes. They are thirsty letters, sometimes sparkling briefly with humor, but always, beneath the busy 'little black words', aching with loss of love and consequently, loss of something singular in his art. Loss of Camille.

As I read the letters through, I find the caviar jar near the bottom of the chest. I hold the jar in my hand. It is long emptied of its savory contents. I roll it in my palm as I read the final letters.

Phrases leap from the pages.

The salutation is always the same, "My darling little girl;" not so little any more, not so young. It is a more proper form of address for Mireilles!

The phrases emerge from the pages.

"I am here in the vicinity of you. If you love me you will come to me. R."

I had accepted the challenge mindlessly. It was mid-June, 1951. Risto had come to the south of France to attend the wedding of his friend Eluard in Saint-Tropez. His being so near me, like some hovering bird, had drawn me again to L'Auberge de Citronnier, like some addict reaching for a fix. I met him, I, who had vowed never to see him again, after learning in 1947 of Jean-Michel, Fabienne's little boy. I learned, again – in June, 1951, there was a second child by Fabienne, a little girl. I returned to Vence in a morass of despondency.

Miri had grown concerned.

"Are you ill, Maman? You are so quiet. You are never like this. Should you see Docteur Robussin?"

I had assured her I was only downcast about some business matters left over from my father's estate. She seemed to accept this.

And Risto? The very next letter was ebullient…seeming to shout from the page.

"A great fanfare for the life that can never separate us?"

This had only made me angry, to have my heart still beat so fast on reading such words.

He has never let me go, yet to him, I am incapable of seeing with his eyes, his eyes so like an instrument, vital to all he is. He thinks I am blind.

Now, all is reversed. This time, he must not see what I see – Mireilles! He must not know what I know. I am afraid for my child.

Risto has never treated his children well. He has treated them with a kind of rich man's neglect, and his artist's preoccupation, leaving little room for love.

He does not try to know them nor does he respect their mothers, dropping the young ones like so many bundles of newspapers upon some street! Occasionally he will show them off as merely another form of creation, or boast to them as he did with Roberto at the Barcelona Museum. He recognizes the blood tie only when he must.

As the darkness begins to streak with a pearly dawn, I gather up the envelopes and grope my way downstairs by the light of the lamp in the corridor to the salon. There is the grate, brimming over with summer greens. Putting the letters upon the floor, I carefully remove the branches and finding the evening newspaper, roll it up, place it in the grate and light it with a match from the kitchen.

Kneeling on the Aubusson rug in orange and blue, the carpet from the house of my father, I pile my envelopes onto the hearth grate, as many as will ignite at one time, fanning them until they glow into flame. Watching them burn, throwing flickering shadows on the stucco walls of the room, I am reminded of Risto's studio at the Château de Chevauchers, where like supplicants in some primitive temple, we had made love in wavering candlelight, the shadow of two lovers cast upon the wall.

I wait until the last inch is burned, and I can break and scatter the mouse-gray dust with the poker. Creeping up the stairs, I repeat the process until all the letters in their blue envelopes are ash, which I distribute evenly on the hearth.

Sitting there before the powdery remains, I think of the Phoenix, the mythical bird, fabled to have burned itself to death, only to rise from its ashes in the freshness of youth to live another life cycle.

All that is left of years of love is a gaping chest, open on my bed upstairs, inside of which are an empty caviar crock, a packet of Risto's drawings, and my attempts at poetry.

I replace the flowers in the grate, when I am sure there is no red ember left. It is getting light and I return to my room. If, in the morning, Miri should say the house smells of smoke, I will tell her she must be dreaming.

On rising the morning after the night of the letterburning, my daughter does notice the smell of smoke, but I am already cooking thick-sliced bacon when she descends the stairs and explain the matches were bad.

"What a smell of sulphur!" I exclaim, opening the kitchen window to the garden, letting in the air, cleansed from the rain of yesterday. She is preparing for a picnic-climb with friends, wrapping bread and cheese and fruit in a damp cloth, putting it in her string bag, readying her sketchbook, and talking excitedly about the day ahead of her.

She gives a deep sigh, while still chewing her bacon.

"The day looks to be clear, but bring a scarf anyway, in case it rains as yesterday," I say, as she runs out the front with a lilting goodbye.

It would seem a normal day, but it is not. Gathering up my string bag, I go to the *poste* where there is a telephone. We do not have one in the stone house. I place a call to Paris. There will be a two-hour wait. In the interim, I go to the bank, withdrawing all my savings, then proceed to the bus terminal and purchase two one-way tickets to Paris. We have to go into Cannes, first, so I reserve seats for the earliest morning bus tomorrow, in order to get the 10:00 o'clock connection to the capital.

Back at the *poste*, my call has come through. It is to the nursing home where my mother is living, in the Montparnasse section of Paris. She has sold the Avenue Victor Hugo house. Maman, only in her mid-60s, has been for the past two years in the nursing home because of a degeneration of the hip-bones, and needs constant care. Olga has been able to accompany her.

Save for the hip affliction, she would be with me. I have begged her to join Mireilles and me often enough. But in her proud way, supported by my father's estate, she prefers the nursing establishment and its attendant society.

She is content, and in spite of my persuasions, she has always refused to live with me, professing it to be a burden, an absurdity after all she has provided for Miri and me.

I speak briefly with her, telling her I will be seeing her in a day or two, with her granddaughter. I can hear the tears in her voice as I hang up.

My plan is to reach Paris, go to a hotel – an inexpensive one – and call Suzelle. Then I will see Maman.

The packing is easy; Miri's light dresses, a sweater or two, a raincoat, some sandals, and the same for myself. The heavier clothes, I pack in an old valise with a broken lid, and in the wooden chest with the brass fittings. Buried at the bottom are the empty crock, my poetry, and a packet of Risto's precious drawings.

I put the two cases in the crawl space under the stairs, knowing that my concierge, from whom I rent by the month, and with whom I am on excellent terms, will permit me to leave them there for an indeterminate period.

I await Miri's return, expecting a whole array of protests. I can hear them now.

"Why must we leave? Is it for long? What about my sketch class? How about the artist who wishes to paint me? Why, Maman? Why?"

I prepare myself for the outcry. *Grand-mère* will be the excuse. It rains again this afternoon, not as hard as yesterday, but enough to dampen the earth and flowers, enough to fill me with resolve, as if my lungs would burst with the fragrance, making me finally certain of everything, especially love.

1953 July Paris

THE HAND OF GOD

26.

I SIT WITH SUZELLE IN the twilight over a glass of wine. We are in her fine house in Neuilly-sur-Seine on the outskirts of Paris. Far below, I can see the gleam of the river as it winds its way from the city to the cleaner reaches of woodland and meadow.

Suzelle and I talk so intensely, we forget to light the lamps.

"Were there other men?" she asks, genuine in her concern.

"One or two. The war decimated my choices, but one or two who might have been important in a different life," I reply. "There was a fat burgher from Lyons…"

Suzelle laughs.

"Then, towards the end of the occupation, a young French soldier I met at the rehabilitation hospital. He was in Vence to recover from some not too severe wounds. A handsome man. He was going to be an accountant!" I laugh. "That did it! Anyway, he seemed to love me."

"But not enough for marriage?"

"It was I who did not love enough."

"Love isn't always necessary."

"For me, it is."

I do not mention Monsieur Bonnard.

Suzelle sips her wine. "Oh, Camille. Why couldn't you have loved him enough!"

"There was always Risto. Once you've had the best – it's impossible to commit to something lesser – at least it is for me. I tried," I say. "Besides, I was happy, in my way. I gave Mireilles a gentle world. Life held for us a serenity, a kind of bitter sweetness. Risto never let me go, you know. I always felt we were like the two lovers in Rodin's Hand of God – twined together forever, held in the giant palm of the almighty – cast in bronze."

"You're fooling yourself, Camille."

I smile into the darkness at Zelle's obtuseness. There is a long silence. Out of it, Suzelle says, "You were just an expression of his libido on canvas – and in bed."

"Careful, Zelle."

"I'm sorry. I can't help saying it. You could have had all this…or something very like it. You threw it all away when you went off with that man."

"I have no regrets."

"What was it like to be his model?" She asks, suddenly curious.

"It was so natural. Art was so much a part of him. Do you know what I mean?"

"No."

"They once called him Protean. Risto could change everything he touched. Some magic in him, some gift for metamorphosis made him paint the way he did. He used everything…including me, I suppose."

"I'm glad you admit it."

"No. No, you don't understand. I went along with it happily. Art was just one of the many things we…did."

"And what of Mireilles?" Zelle says, changing the subject. "What about her? Have you ever thought it might be selfish on your part, not to marry – for her sake? To give her a father – at least the image of one?"

"Selfish?"

"Yes. Selfish."

"Selfish, not to marry a man I didn't love? Selfish, when I love another?"

Zelle gets up, goes to the decanter, and pours herself more wine. She gestures with the crystal vessel toward my glass. I shake my head.

"Does she know the truth?"

"She does not," I respond through compressed lips.

"She has missed a father, and a famous one."

"She'll survive."

"One hopes so," Suzelle says, ominously. "Why haven't you explained it to her? She's old enough to understand."

"There are good reasons."

"But she would want to know him."

"Please, Zelle," I interrupt.

"And Risto doesn't even realize she exists? Now, that's amazing!"

"He's not known for his paternalism," I say wryly. "Besides there is no need for him – or her to know. She is content believing in the father who is dead – a good man who cared for her."

"And the truth?"

"Truth isn't reason enough," I say, "Although…"

"Although?"

"The reason I came running to Paris is because I think Risto approached her on the street in Cannes…wanted to do her portrait."

"What?"

"I was terrified. Miri came home and told me. Risto was in the south at the time."

"Good Lord, Camille, doesn't this tell you something?" Suzelle was pacing, agitated.

"It was a shock, but I cannot tell Miri. I cannot tell Risto. I want no claim on him. All the others have clung to him, like lichens on a rock. To tell Miri would require an explanation for my whole early life with Risto…how we met…rue La Boëtie…What would she think of me? Besides, Risto would be no father to her now."

"Perhaps you do him a disservice."

"Have you ever seen a child in his work? No! – a nude woman or an abstract structure or a scene of war or a bull-fight, but never a child with a ball or a toy, or heaven forbid, with its mother!" I say vehemently.

Suzelle is silent, but she still paces the floor.

"I know it sounds grandiose, but I feel an…immortality because I am the subject of so many of his pictures."

"Don't get carried away," Suzelle interjects.. "But, Camille, you never know. Mireilles might be proud of both her father <u>and</u> her mother!"

"I will not take that chance."

"You think she'll never discover the truth? The two of them meeting in Cannes must give you pause. Talk about 'The Hand of God'. It certainly was a trick of fate."

I shake my head.

"Someday Miri may learn it from a stranger – a chance remark. After all, you did live for nine years with that man. It would be a terrible shock!"

"It won't happen!"

"It is more likely than not to happen," Suzelle says firmly. "And with all this 'immortality' of yours through his paintings, it's highly possible. Did you know there is a mystery about you? There is talk in Paris about exactly who the lady in his famous <u>Dream</u> sequence is. You haven't been in Paris for a long time, so perhaps you're not aware of it. Wait a minute. I want to show you something."

She leaves the verandah, returning with a newspaper clipping. "I saved this for you. I was going to send it to you. Now, I'm almost afraid to show it to you."

The clipping is a critique on the retrospective of Risto's work at Vollard's on rue Lafitte this past June. The model in the <u>Dream</u> sequence is likened to the Duchess of Alba, Goya's supposed mistress at the beginning of the 19th century.

Goya is said to have painted that lady as the <u>Naked Maja</u>. He also painted a second picture exactly the same, only the model is clothed – <u>Vestida</u> – designed to be hung over the nude version in the interests of propriety.

"Of course, Risto's style is at a world removed from Goya's," the critic had written. "The similarity of the two is in the pose of a reclining nude young woman and in the passionate execution. Most striking is the similarity of the mystery of the model. Just who is Goya's beauty? Is she really the Duchess of Alba? And who is Risto's beauty? Is the lady still alive!"

I had no idea just how 'immortal' I have become. Risto's fame had lain dormant during the war period at least until he joined the Communist Party. Most of the artistic life of France had lain fallow during the occupation, with the heel of the boot upon its neck. In the late 40s, there had been a resurgence, and admiration for Risto's work had taken on new life.

Curiosity about the mystery of the lady of the Dream series of paintings – Girl Reclining, Girl Sleeping, Nude Asleep, Dream Entrance - is strong. This work from the early 30s is considered his most beautiful to date. There is growing public desire to know the identity of the lady who posed for Risto for such a long time and whom he painted so sensuously.

"And your poetry is quite famous too, don't forget," Suzelle says, breaking into my thoughts.

"My poems have nothing to do with my life with Risto."

"Don't they?"

"I never mention him in the verses – not once – not directly."

"Tell me, honestly. Could you have written such words without your passion for him?" Suzelle asks.

"Probably not."

"People can put two and two together."

With these final warning words from Suzelle, we turn to talk of other things but my mind races with baleful thoughts beneath our conversation. A cold, rational reality of Miri and me is setting in.

Suddenly, I want to be free, free of a burden I have carried for over 18 years. It is time for the Phoenix, time for new hope; time for courage.

It is time for the truth.

1953 August Cannes

TRUTH

27.

I HAVE ARRANGED TO MEET with Risto on August 25th at L'Auberge du Citronnier. Mireilles will be with me. The pressure of discovery seems to press from underneath. Better to tell the story my way than have some extraneous force bring down the teetering structure I have erected.

My evening spent with Suzelle at her house in Neuilly-sur-Seine had been a revelation. Upon returning to the room in the hotel on the rue Cambon, I had looked at my daughter in her bed, the daughter I have kept in the dark all these years.

It was well after midnight. She had been sound asleep, her tanned face intensely brown against the white of the pillow slip, her breathing even and serene after a tiring day of exploration of the Louvre and the Jeu de Paume, the special Louvre annex, consecrated to the Impressionist painters she so adored.

I gazed at her for a long time with overwhelming fondness. Soon, she would know the story, with the subsequent fabrication on my part. Soon, that tranquil sleep would be disturbed by my past. In telling her the facts of our lives I risked a new hostility that would emerge toward a woman she might never come to trust again.

A decision of years had been reversed this night as I left Suzelle's, riding through the dark streets of Paris in a bouncing taxi, in turmoil, with my friend's words, her thoughts, tormenting my heart. Suzelle had brought to light the horrifying thought that Risto might find Miri again, and not knowing she was his child, work his will and his considerable charm upon an inexperienced and passionate girl so much like her mother.

Now, Miri and I are home in the little stone house in Vence. We have been back since Ausust 1st. Immediately on my return, I had written Risto at his new studio on the rue de Grands-Augustins in Paris. Fabienne is gone and living somewhere in Brittany with their two children. Apparently, he has become intrigued with a Greek model of dubious character. I had learned all this on my sojourn to Paris.

I had received an exuberant response to my request for a meeting with him. In all the years, it was the first time I had asked him for a rendezvous. He was elated, and agreed to meet me toward the end of the month – August 25th – because he had to be in London earlier – an exhibition at the Whitechapel Gallery there.

His final words held a threat or a promise of both. "You have no idea what I have in store for you!" and accompanying the letter was an erotic drawing of a nude man and woman.

You have no idea, Risto, what I have in store for you!

Miri is entranced by the thought of an excursion, "To stay in Cannes overnight, Maman? How marvelous! We can look at all the people! We can stuff ourselves with pralines! We can swim for two whole days!"

"Might get a bit soggy, don't you think?" I reply, as lightly as can.

We arrive at the inn in Cannes one day before Risto's expected arrival. Madame Jacques de Brantes, Jeanne, has given me the usual room over the courtyard as white and pristine as ever. At dinner in the saffron dining room, where Miri and I order the lobster-like crayfish in a delicate sauce, the younger Madame de Brantes is obviously curious about the girl who is my companion.

She gazes constantly at Miri's face, which makes me uncomfortable. She even tries to listen to our words or to engage in conversation about something as simple as the weather. I quickly ask for the check and exclaim, "Let's go out along La Croisette to walk off our dinner," to which my daughter remarks, "What dinner, Maman? You have eaten nothing."

As we stroll the esplanade before the elegant hotels, I am thankful for the tourists that meander too, for they occupy Miri totally. She comments on a costume, a strange hair-do, the new metallic earrings, a bronze body, remarks demanding little response from me.

Next day, it is misty. Miri spends the afternoon on the balcony painting the lemon tree in the courtyard through the soft fog.

"The light is strange…almost yellow," she says. "It's hard to catch it…better use more wash…" she continues talking to herself, dripping the chrome in bright drops on the wooden floor of the balcony.

'Careful!" I say, in a sharp voice.

"Don't worry, Maman." She looks at me hard. "It comes up with water. Why are you so nervous? Don't you want to read or something?"

I pick up Cannes Matin, and pretend to absorb myself in it. The afternoon wears thin, still misty and yellow-gray when suddenly, I hear Miri laugh.

"A man just ran across the courtyard…Lord, he was in a hurry." She is leaning over the railing as I hear the footsteps, his footsteps, on the stairs.

The door is flung open, and Risto is before me in the doorway, eyes gleaming, smile broad and excited, and with a loud "Cammy," he comes to me arms outstretched. I put my finger to my lips in a gesture to silence. So forceful is the motion, he stops abruptly in mid-step, a look of alarm upon his face and an explosive, "*Dieu*, what is it?"

Mireilles has come in to stand in the open doorway to the balcony, flanked by the leaded glass doors. I am between her and Risto and, for a moment, feel like a trapped animal. "How are you Risto?" I say lamely.

"Risto?" exclaims Miri. "The artist? Are you really him? I can't believe it!" She moves toward him and coming from the direction of what light there is on this yellow-gray day, Risto backs away.

"Who is it?" he says, almost at the door, retreating from this onrushing young woman. "I can't see…the light…"

"Maman, I had no idea you knew him."

"Let's sit down," I say firmly, surprised at the control with which I say it. I sit on a corner of the bed. Risto finds the straight chair and, as obedient as a dog, sits there. Miri alone stands.

There is dead silence.

Finally, I say to him, "I'd like you to meet Mireilles, my daughter."

"Your child, Cammy...your daughter?" he asks dumbfounded. "You never told me you had a child."

"You never asked."

"Whom did you marry? How could you have never told me?"

Risto studies Miri for a long time. She stands before him, mesmerized by his presence and his fame.

"She is like you," he says slowly. "The curving cheek line...the nose...I have seen this girl before...earlier this summer...she attracted me then...reminded me of you at 17. I can't believe this..." He sits on the chair, crumpled and uncomfortable.

Miri and Risto stare at one another with an un-admitted recognition. Each is immobile. Each seems suddenly aware of a tie between them.

Miri speaks. "Then it was you...you approached me...in July...to paint me...didn't you? It was you, wasn't it?"

Risto nods.

"But how do you know Maman?"

"I have always known your mother...since she was your age," he responds.

"But where? How?" Turning to me, her expression one of watching some play enacted, Miri says, "I never knew you knew such a great artist. Why didn't you tell me? I would have loved to meet him." She pauses and then cannily asks, "Is it because I met him on the street we ran away so quickly?"

"Perhaps," I mumble.

"But why, Maman? You acted afraid. I never saw you quite like that."

"Come on, Cammy," Risto interjects rising from his chair. "This is ridiculous. You have been keeping secrets."

"There were reasons perhaps you, at least, will understand. I'm not sure that Miri will."

"Don't speak of me as if I'm not even in the room!" she exclaims angrily, standing next to Risto.

"Come on, Cammy…out with it," he says.

My audience of two is alive with anticipation. I look at them, standing side by side, father and daughter, similar in stance, in color, in the eyes, and regarding them levelly, I finally say, "Mireilles is your child, Risto."

"What did you say?"

"You heard me," I respond to him.

"I heard you too," Miri says with a wail.

"You are father and daughter."

Risto lets out an oath of disbelief, goes back to the chair and sinks onto it, shaking his head. Miri is still and white.

"This is incredible, Cammy. I don't believe this."

"You can believe it."

"I can't," Miri cries.

"Why have you never told me, Cammy?" he cries out.

"I was afraid I'd be just another one of those mother and baby combinations you abandon along your path," I say rather bitterly.

Risto looks shocked.

"You think I'm so uncaring?"

"Of maternity, yes."

"You've deprived me of the joy of knowing this girl – my girl – even of her existence? All these years? And what of her? What she and I have lost?" He is becoming purple with anger under the tan. "You stripped me of my rights without my even knowing it."

"And what of me?" my daughter whispers.

I go to her. "You have no idea of the circumstance. I didn't want you to suffer for my early life."

"You strung me along with the story of a dead father, when all the time I could have known a real live one…one of my own," she says vehemently. "You must have loved him. Why didn't you let me?"

"You've cheated us both," Risto says coldly. He moves close to Miri.

"There was no way I could tell either of you. Miri, you don't know Risto."

"Of course I don't! How could I," she says, turning to me.

"Camille, I never knew you. I thought I did, but obviously, I never did," Risto says in a low voice. He moves out to the balcony.

Miri sits in Risto's chair, her face hostile. "It was a long affair?"

"My lifetime long."

"You have loved him your whole life?"

"Yes. I was your age when I met him. There has never been any other. Not really. You know that."

"And our name 'Aristide', Maman? Did you just make it up?"

"Ruy Aristide is Risto's natal name."

"Ruy Aristide," she repeats softly to herself.

"He took 'Risto' from the name Aristide...It was his nickname as a child...also he used it for the effect," I say clumsily.

"You two were never married."

"No."

"So I am...a bastard."

I nod in response.

She weeps, quietly at first, then in gusts, which take a long moment to subside. I look into the dripping eyes, yearning to be admitted there.

"Why, we might have been a family if you'd only told the truth," she says brokenly, her breath tattered.

"Never, Miri."

"It's all been a lie," she mumbles. "My whole life, a lie,..my mother, a lie...my father..." Then, jumping to her feet she runs to the balcony. I hear her call, "Risto...Monsieur...Papa." I glimpse them through the open doorway as they stand at the iron railing, looking intensely at one another.

"Take me away with you," I hear her say. "Now. Let me be with you for a little while. Let me know you and learn from you. Do you know I want to be an artist?"

And the deep voice answering, "Yes. Yes. Of course you'll come with me. An artist? Really? You want to be an artist?"

'They' are going. Without me. 'They' are leaving me alone. The last thing I hear as the two brush past me like shadows, stirring the wind as they pass, is their whispering voices.

"Yes, now!" the voice low and "Please, Papa," the voice girlish, and finally last of all, as the door closes behind them, "Papa, do you suppose there is any way in heaven, I might have inherited just a bit of your talent?"

1954 September Cannes

ALONE

28.

I HAVE BEEN ALONE NOW for over a year. Last summer, after the loss of Miri – after the loss of Risto – I returned to Vence to the little stone house to find it achingly empty.

Suddenly, I am called to Paris. Maman, deathly ill, drifted off from me and died in peace, forcing me deeper into the helpless melancholy in which I find myself. I grow more isolated and alone. Even dear Monsieur Héberd has passed away, his bookstore now in the possession of his nephew. Suzelle, at whose house I am staying, tries desperately to drag me from the mire of despondency, but 'I told you so' is implicit in her gaze.

I finally decide there is only one place I want to be; the south of France at L'Auberge du Citronnier. Even the pain of the final encounter there had paled in comparison to the fact of love experienced in that sweet venue. The shadow of a young girl in the moonlight passing beneath the lemon tree had been me after all. It cost me much to admit that the inn is my only way to forge a link to 'them'.

I return to the inn. It is September. I bring but one valise and my wooden chest with brass corners, certain Risto would be gone from Cannes this late in the season, giving me a chance to test myself against memory. Madame Jeanne de Brantes, the younger, gave me the same room with the balcony. I asked for it, perhaps a mistake, because the pristine look I had always admired now seemed only cold.

The same room. The same La Croisette. The same sea. The same wooden raft. The same Basso's but no one to join me. Monsieru Bonnard is gone. Risto is...oh, I don't know, somewhere with her, my Miri. There is more anguish to this 'her', than ever could be if he had a lover.

When I first arrive, I swim to the raft. The sea is cold. Instead, I walk along its edge, watching the salty water cream against my toes. I gaze at the pewter-colored bills above Cannes. There are no elemental figures standing there as Risto meant there to be.

They think me strange at L'Auberge du Citronnier. I eat so little. In the evening, I prefer to take a few cold shrimp and some cheese to my room. I avoid the dining room, which I have enlivened in the past and where I so relished the *cuisine* in that other life.

One windy, clear day, upon my regular afternoon walk through the town, a week after my appearance at the inn, I stop before the window of the confectioner's shop. It is near the quai. I am not really seeing the glistening array of dipped chocolates and marzipan behind the pane, when suddenly I am aware of the shadow of two people passing, the double image in the glass catching my eye. When I finally turn, I see the two backs, one so young with shiny blonde hair, the other, short and strong with hair quite silver.

Miri and Risto seem deeply absorbed in conversation as they disappear around the corner, she bowing to him, almost subservient. In panic, I retreat to the safety of the lemon tree, panting quickly all the way, yet elated because the link to 'them' is forged.

Why are they here? It is already autumn. Why have they not returned to Paris? I discover why the very next morning, for in Cannes Matin, I see a large advertisement for an exhibition in the art section of the paper.

Mireilles Aristide is to show a collection of water colors at the Aucliffe Galerie on rue Menton, the cross street, next to Basso's, the show to last for two weeks. My inn is benefitting from a full house. Even this late in the season, a large number of boats and yachts remain in the *vieux port* for the event, sponsored as it is by Miri's irresISTible father.

Risto's name looms large in the advertisement. The mother of the girl – Mireilles Aristide – remains unknown, only adding to the excitement and much speculation as to her identity seems to whisper down the hall of the inn and laugh at the small, oak bar.

I am determined to see the exhibition at all costs, not at the opening, of course. Finally, late of a chilly afternoon after it has been on view for 13 of its run of 14 days, I manage to slip in just before the Galerie closes for the night.

I have carefully inspected the Aucliffe Galerie on a daily basis from a vantage point on Basso's cold terrace at one of the small tables right next to the entrance door of the restaurant. I sit alone each late afternoon over a small glass of wine, watching from across the street, until I see Risto and Miri leave.

I devour their images, as finally the pink globes along the avenue are lit. I watch my daughter. She looks older. So does he.

The afternoon before the last day of the exhibition, I see the two leave early in noisy joviality with a group of people, and they disappear.

I enter the portals of Aucliffe Galerie. I walk slowly into its center. It is hung with over 30 watercolors and drawings by Miri. Only three other people are present; a young man with a beard, and a lady with a small girl by the hand. There is nothing to disturb me except the pictures themselves.

I have read all the reviews. Miri's work has been generally admired, but too often compared to the mature work of her father rather unfairly. However, I find the exhibition remarkable. The drawings are clear and clean; the forms well shaped in charcoal; the watercolors blaze with force and character.

The exhibition is numbered and laid out by date, so I have the luxury of reviewing the interior life my daughter has led through the past year. I stop before the first, a lyrical depiction of the Mediterranean, but it is without tree, flower, animal, or person. It is a view...a still life... with no life.

I find that all the early pictures, drawn and painted with such care, are strangely stark, and in spite of the lively pigments, there is something infinitely sad in she who painted them.

By picture number 11, there is the beginning of a change. It was painted last December and is of the studio Risto now uses in Paris. It is a familiar scene to me, because in the center of the painting, is the couch – covered in cretonne, now with yellow roses printed upon it.

By number 17, there is a picture of a little girl. The child's eyes are wistful. And 18, the child is running along a stretch of yellow sand; 19, perched on a gray rock by the sea, but her face is lifted to the sun. Miri is beginning to reach for the warmth.

By number 20, there is a picture of a woman sitting on a stiff chair against a wall. She wears a blue dress so like one of my own, the tilt of the head, anguished. 22, is a picture of a woman lying face down upon the sand, as if reading something into the individual granules beneath her. The, at last, 28 and 29 are both of a woman in a garden, again in that French blue dress, only now there are tomatoes and pimentos and eggplant growing all around her. It is my garden at Vence. The woman has her head up. She's smiling. That woman is me.

And I know I am forgiven.

DÉJA VU

29.

I THINK OF MIRI IN Paris with Risto. I think of him, of 'them'. Still, I have been living my life at L'Auberge du Cirtonnier with a measure of content, convinced of my child's forgiveness, and aware from the paintings in her exhibition last September, that she too thinks of me. I am even able to write a little poetry.

It is a misty and cold November. The hills and woodlands above Cannes seem made of silver. This particular evening, I walk by the sea, until fingers chilled, I return to my white room at the inn. I rub my hands together, making them tingle and pour myself a tot of cognac.

It is about 6:00 o'clock. There is a tap on my door, an unusual occurrence. The maid always knocks, but that is in the morning. I go to the door cautiously, then, open it wide. My breath is taken away. Before me stands Miri.

It has been a year and three months since I have seen her face to face. I inspect her intently as I used to do when she came back from hectic play, looking for damage. There is dead silence as I gaze hungrily at the face of my child, no longer a child. Her face is thinner the dark eyes wiser.

"May I come in, Maman?" The voice is low.

"Oh, Miri…Please."

She comes in shyly, removing a heavy, cable knit sailor's cardigan. She is wearing a plaid skirt, a white shirtwaist, and knit stockings.

"It's getting so cold."

"Yes," I say eagerly, fearful the apparition will dissolve. "Yes it is... Would you like a little cognac?"

"No...no...yes."

"Please sit down."

She moves uncertainly to the corner of the bed and lowers herself upon it. I pour the drink for her into a glass and present it to her. Our fingers make contact for a moment, but it is enough to make me draw back my hand too quickly, spilling the drops of amber liquid onto the plaid skirt.

"Oh, I'm so sorry..." I say, dabbing at the skirt with a towel from a nearby chair.

"No, no, Maman. Really it's all right."

I am standing before her. I do not know what to do with myself. I twist the towel in my hands. Finally, hesitant, I turn and sit between the windows on the stiff-backed chair on which Risto has sat so many times.

"I'm glad to see you," I manage to say. "You look well...a bit older, perhaps, but it becomes you." I smile at her tenderly. "You're thinner too...perhaps that's it. Anyway, the effect is...very pretty." It sounds feeble, for I find her breathtakingly beautiful. She is my child.

"I'm glad too, Maman. I've...missed you."

"You have? Really? You don't know how much I longed to see you." I rise from the chair and turn my back to her so she will not see the uncontrollable working of my mouth.

"Maman?" She is behind me. I feel the light touch of her hand upon my shoulder and before I know it, we are in each other's arms. I cannot stop hugging her. I pat her shoulder, touch her face, pull her again to me. There are no words.

Then, very softly, I hear "I love you, Maman."

My joy is limitless. In seconds, I seem to have retrieved all I had lost. There is life. There is love. There is Mireilles, and she has come home to me.

"Oh, my child. I love you too."

We hug again and finally break apart.

I sit beside her on the corner of the bed. I am happier than I have been since the early days in Vence, when we were creating a life together, interdependent and sure.

"Tell me. Tell me everything."

"I'll try."

Before she can speak, my own words pour out.

"I saw your exhibition. You're painting beautifully. I was so proud, you've no idea. And the pictures...they're so much you. Looking at them...well, it was like being with you for a moment."

"You saw them? I was there every day. I didn't see you."

"No, I waited until I saw you leave. I didn't want to embarrass you."

"We...Papa...We had dinner downstairs. Madame de Brantes...She told us you were living here."

"I'm so thankful she did."

"That was three weeks ago."

"So long?"

"You don't know how many times I've walked down rue Mistral, hoping to see you as by accident." Her words are tumbling now. "I've hidden under the lemon tree and looked up at the balcony and the lighted windows behind the railing. Sometimes I saw your shadow. Sometimes there was moonlight. Sometimes it was drizzling...and cold."

"Oh, I wish I'd known. But that's over now...isn't it, Miri?"

"It's over."

"What I did...what I kept from you. It had nothing to do with anything except my loving you so much. I wanted to protect you."

"At first, I was so angry. It was the shock...and I understood nothing. I had to find out for myself."

Miri rises. It always amazes me how an inanimate room can take on life and passion because of the people inside it.

"How is your...father?"

She shakes her head, then starts to speak, slowly at first, her voice troubled, gaining in speed and rising as she tells her story.

"In the beginning...a year ago last September...it was magic. Papa....You know how gay he can be. I went back with him to Paris to the house on rue de Grands-Augustins. There was a studio downstairs with tons of pictures and sculptures, and so fascinating." She pauses.

"Papa gave me the little room right next to it...cleared it out himself. It smelled of turpentine and oil paint, but it had a window in the stone wall. He put a bed in there and I felt content," she continues, "except for you, Maman. It took me a long time to forgive you...for keeping me from this exciting man who was my father. I just didn't understand."

"How could you?"

"He seemed so perfect. He let me watch him work...helped me with criticism. I painted right alongside him. He liked what I did... but...well..." She bows her head. "There was a lady that lived with him upstairs. She was pretty...but sort of...trashy...you know what I mean?"

I nod. Indeed I do.

"She treated me like some sort of wicked step child...ordered me around...hated when Papa would include me in his dinner plans or took me with them to the theater. And the trouble was, he listened to her... he would get...mean with me if I seemed to, oh, I don't know, interfere. I tried not to. I really tried to stay out of their way."

"She was jealous of you."

"Jealous? But why should HE be mean?" She sits beside me.

"Perhaps you made him feel old...or maybe she picked on him about you when they were alone."

"She certainly picked on him about something! It got to be every other night. I could hear them fighting upstairs...so loud...I used to put a pillow over my head, and Maman, I began to long for the way we used to live. Somehow those days in Vence seemed to have been heaven, and what I was living, turned into something ugly." She looks up at me.

"Then we came back here for most of the summer, to the villa off La Croisette. It was more or less the same arrangement – no better – maybe worse. She made me feel so unwanted. Papa knew I was unhappy, I'll say that for him." She looks down at her hands. A teardrop splashes on the young skin of her wrist.

Then, she says, "He only arranged the show at Aucliffe to appease me."

"I don't believe that, Miri, certainly not just to appease you. It was a wonderful show."

"It was exciting, Maman, no?" I see the tip of a smile, and I respond with the widest one I can muster.

"The most exciting day of my life was looking at your pictures at the Aucliffe Galerie…next to the day you were born."

"After the show in September," she continues, "we went back to Paris. This time, there was a big difference."

I can hardly hear her.

"The lady still lived with Papa upstairs, but he had found…a new little model he was using. Morgana, the lady upstairs, knew what was going on, but of course, I didn't, not until…until…one day, I came home unexpectedly. My sketch class had been cancelled. I walked into the studio, and there on the couch…you know the flowered couch he always says was his trademark? There they were, the new model and Papa…naked together."

"Ah, Miri, Miri…"

"Maman…the girl, the new model…she was younger than me, much younger…maybe 16. It seemed so savage what they were doing to each other." Miri's voice becomes hushed. "Papa only looked up from what he was doing. His face was funny, kind of distorted, and he was…naked, you know." Her voice turns ragged. "His bottom…was so white, compared to the brown of his legs. It matched his hair," she says with a shudder.

I have to turn away from my daughter. I cannot bear the expression on her face.

"Papa..he just looked at me and said, 'Get out. Haven't you enough sense to get out?' I must have been standing there for some minutes. I couldn't move, and the girl. She looked so pleased with herself…so victorious."

"Ah, Miri."

"How could he…with practically…a little girl?"

"He could. He does."

"It disgusts me!"

"It's his nature."

"Are all men like that?"

"Hardly." I laugh a little laugh.. "Some would like to be, though." I pause. "What did you do then?"

"Well," she says, "I had some money in my pocket, and I found a taxi, and I went to Tante Suzells's house. She knew I was in Paris. I had talked to her on the phone. I had said some mean things about you, Maman, but it was the way I felt at the time. She was home luckily, and she took me in, gave me enough money and clothes to come down here on the train and look for you. But when I got to Cannes, who was waiting for me in the station but Papa. He had taken an airplane."

"How did he know you'd be in Cannes?"

"Tante Suzelle told him. He knew she was the only person I knew in Paris and must have called her when I stormed out of the studio. She convinced him to come down here and get me and find you and work it out."

"Suzelle!"

"We came here to the inn for dinner. God, what a meal! I didn't want to talk to him. I hated looking at him. All I could see was the way he was in the studio." She is silent, then, "I'm sure he knows where I am." It's a declaration I am not sure I want.

"Yes. He probably realizes you are here with me, by now."

Miri is growing angry. "He's been keeping such an eye on me, afraid I'll bolt, and he has been trying to make things up to me, by arranging another exhibition. He re-rented the same villa off La Croisette, only it's just him and me right now, no girl friend...yet." She shakes her head. "It's very strained...unreal...He talks to me about how his energy requires that kind of 'refueling'. It makes no sense to me! I paint. I feel an artist, but I certainly don't run after little boys!"

I have to laugh. "Of course not, but everyone is different, and this has been the pattern of your father ever since I've known him. I think... you know what I think? It's his ego. A young girl makes him feel young again."

"He talks about you. He always loved you. It's about the only thing in him I respect."

"Oh, now Miri! Not the only thing."

"Well…his art."

"Other things too."

"Perhaps, but Maman. I can't go back to the villa."

"You don't have to. You'll stay here with me."

"Maman. Everything you did…not telling me about him. It all makes sense to me now. Imagine! I thought we could have been a family. It would have been a disaster!"

Miri has recovered somewhat. Her voice is stronger. "What if he finds us!" she exclaims with alarm.

"He will. Of course he will."

"What shall we do?" She looks at me in panic.

"Nothing."

"Nothing?"

I merely smile, kiss her on the cheek and move to the bureau and my powder puff. Tonight no cold meal in my bedroom! No indeed. Tonight we will eat downstairs in full view of whomever should happen to come to L'Auberge du Citronnier and dine on their excellent *cuisine*!

1954 November and Beyond Cannes

AND SO WE LIVE

30.

RISTO FINDS US THE next day. It is a day filled with the sound of mournful fog horns from the sea.

At first, he finds only me. Miri has gone to the art store for a new supply of sketch paper and charcoal. She had slept well, after we had eaten in the dining room, truffled terrine and grilled turbot, with red carnations in a copper bowl between us. She cuddled close to me in the huge white bed. I could barely sleep. My spirit was so transcendent, so of a piece, I could only watch her face, hear her light breaths against the pillow through the night.

We breakfasted on *café au lait, croissants,* and black raspberry jam in our room. Madame de Brantes, the younger, brought it to us with the traditional rose on the tray. She could see our happiness. I knew her natural curiosity was at the bursting point.

Risto finally comes to my door and finds me alone in the room. I know by the sound of his footsteps on the stairs, the pounding step I had heard so often and await with love and trepidation. I am only calm.

I throw open the door to my room, on first hearing his steps and am sitting in the straight chair between the tall windows to the balcony awaiting him. He stands framed in the doorway, his face somber and dark.

"Where is she?" It's his opening remark as his eyes search the room.

"Can't you even say hello?"

He glares at me. "I want to see Mireilles."

"She's not here."

"Then I'll wait," and because there is no other chair in the room, he sits on the bed. There is silence. Finally, he asks, "Where'd she go?"

"To the art supply shop."

"She's got plenty of supplies," he says grumpily.

"Not here, she hasn't."

He shoots me a glance of such anger, in the old days I would have trembled. Not today. There is a muted hoot from an offshore fog horn.

"We'll see," he says.

Since our daughter will be returning before long, I decide to bring up wounds.

"Miri told me the reason for her sudden departure from your studio in Paris."

Risto's face seems to expand in confusion.

"She's a very naïve young woman."

"Oh, yes. She is. And you are a particularly sophisticated man." I let the word 'sophisticated' hang in the air. It is such a ridiculous description of his behavior.

"Her biggest shock was that your partner was so young."

Again, I let the word 'partner' hang. "She couldn't get over the girl being younger than she. That bothered her most."

Risto says nothing but his face has that odd, confused look. Then, "She's got to grow up."

"Don't worry. She is doing so rapidly. You've been seeing to that." My voice is dry. "I think she now understands why we three could never live together."

"Humph," is the response.

"Risto, she is more comfortable with me."

He looks at me sharply and then begins to speak, feelings overlapping, words half swallowed.

"That's ridiculous. She has been thrilled living with me. Just look at her art. Oh, you haven't seen it."

"But I have. The exhibition…"

"She's developed so, don't you agree? She's becoming so strong. Her linear expression is remarkable in one so young."

I always forget Risto is first of all the artist. He is on his feet, walking the floor, side-tracked by his passion. "I want to teach her more about the use of color, the use of people and animals and live things..." He stops. "I don't want you to think that's all there is to it, just art," he says, noticing my quizzical expression. "We paint together. We've been to the bullfights, and I've taught her to swim out farther even than the raft. You remember the raft? We cook together. She knew nothing about cleaning fish or making a *bourride* or a *cassoulet*!"

"I always did it."

"No matter. She's a spirited girl, who needs badly a man around her...a father. She's only had women in her life – you, her grandmother, little girls at school, her Tante Suzelle." He winces when he says the name.

"That was all I had at her age."

"You had your father." He pauses.

"True," I say.

"You had me."

"Did I?"

"You know you did! Look, Camille. Miri has been isolated," he continues, "living in a little town like Vence, in a world so remote. She needs exposure. It is one thing I can give her."

"You have already given her plenty of exposure!" I interrupt.

"That was only a single incident. I can assure you it won't happen again. And she just stood there! For God's sake, what was I to do?"

"I'm sure I don't know."

"No...well, I don't either, Cammy," using my name in the old affectionate version.

"I can give her so much." He is before me in the sullen-boy stance I have so often seen. "Don't you see? I have money. I can take her to Spain and Italy, even America. She can see the world. She can meet the greatest artists of our day, be with people who will stimulate her, help her grow. There is so much I can teach her, give her, that you can't – not because you are inadequate. On the contrary! You've raised alone a perfectly wonderful girl, but you're not in the same position as I, Cammy. You've had her all these years. Now it's my turn."

Before I can answer, I am aware there is another person in the room. She is there, standing framed in the doorway, as her father had been a moment ago. I do not know how long she has been standing there. Neither Risto nor I had heard her step upon the stair, so concentrated were we in trying to reach each other beneath the words. We turn to her, expectant, our voices stilled.

Miri looks solemn, standing there quietly. Finally, from the door, she asks,

"Have I no choice?"

It is said so simply, Risto and I stumble all over ourselves to reassure her that, indeed, she has a choice, the ultimate choice.

She comes into the room. It feels crowded with the three of us there. "The problem is, I need you both. No…don't touch me," for we have both moved toward her.

"I didn't go to the art store. I've been walking along the beach looking out into the mist. The water looked like mercury."

She stands in the middle of the room between Risto and me, her face thoughtful.

"I'll be 19 in January, only weeks away. I think it's time I tried life on my own."

"Come back with me to Paris. We'll have a showing there…"

"No, Papa. I can't live with you."

"Of course you can."

"No. I don't fit into your life. And I never would have. Maman didn't."

Risto turns red.

"Oh, Papa. Please understand. I want to see you…be part of your world. But I can't live with you. Nor you, Maman," she says gently to me. "You would keep me a child. I want both of you, and that means living with neither."

Both Risto and I, again, move toward her.

"No," Miri escapes us and moves to a vantage point near the French doors. "I need both of you. It can't just be one or the other. I am both of you. If I'm alone, live alone and see you both, the two pieces of me can finally come together."

Risto and I are silent. It is quite a declaration, and I realize that in all the tug of war that has transpired, I have been selfish. I've not considered Miri's needs, only mine. As for Risto, he has never ever been able to think of any but his own.

* * *

It comes about, Miri's desire to emerge as whole. Through Risto's Cannes connections, she rents a little apartment here in Cannes on the rue de Plage (which is nowhere near the beach), consisting of one room at the back on the ground floor of a very old stucco building with enough space for her easel and a large closet to store her art supplies. She is now beginning to work in oils, a challenge to her skills.

With my help, we find an old brass bed in an ancient barn and persuade the farmer's wife to sell it to us, polish it to a gleaming shine, buy a gas grill and some cooking pots and Miri is established. She is only a short walk from me down La Croisette. We see each other often.

She has discovered a young man from Marseille who works on a fishing boat, of which he owns one half. He plans to run a whole fleet one day. She met him on a Sunday after Noël, while sketching sea birds on the quai, now a regular and constant rendezvous whenever he is in port. He is wind-swept and passionate, and the only time I was present at one of their meetings, his dark blue eyes never left my daughter's face.

I have a permanent room on a yearly basis at L'Auberge du Citronnier. The room has become my home, no longer so pristine, with my sewing spools, powder box, writing materials, the Aubusson rug upon the wooden floor, and my Bonnard glowing upon the wall between the French doors.

I am writing again, my poems, now small character studies. One I call 'Portrait of the Artist'. Another, 'Still Life', describes the stone house in Vence I knew and loved and the woman who lived inside.

Risto? He shuttles between Paris and Cannes. I haven't seen him in two months because it's still winter, but when he comes to me, he is full of ardor, bursting with 'art'. Sometimes he seeks my advice and counsel, and I am forced to say with a trace of a smile, "Oh, Risto, *chèri. Tais-toi* – just be quiet and paint!"

Spring will be upon us soon and Risto will come back.

He always has.